SAVAGE SPEAR

OF THE UNICORN

STORIES BY

DELICIOUS TACOS

For Dad

Should Have Let Them Fire Me

Someone snitched. One of you? You did me a favor. Should have let them fire me. That fucking new office, a closet, no window, no space, trapped. I mean who cares, my world is my computer. I should have let them fire me. I didn't want to tinker with shit, change shit. Can't work just to do more work anymore. Should have let them fire me. What if I could have got severance. A hundred grand…

I should– I mean, they called me out and I acted honestly. Spiritually. I cravenly tried to keep my job but it's not even that. I really don't want to fuck my workplace over. America's Leaders in Consumer Packaged Goods don't want to employ a crack smoking would be high school girl molesting menace. My stupid hobby could harm people's livelihoods. On the other hand who fucking cares.

Should have threatened to sue. You can't fire me in California. Lawful off duty activity. Then again I confessed to felonies. Talked about wanting to fuck 15 year old girls. You do too so shut the fuck up. I did tweet fireable offenses on the clock. Could have got past that deleting Twitter. Anyway that's not why they said they'd fire me. It was for the blog. Which I wrote on off hours. Unlike my previous job where I wrote instead of working. But what if I can never work again. What if I want a wife. A kid. You need a recommendation.

So what. Disgusted with myself. A coward. I should have walked off and I didn't. Afraid about money. Having to move. Losing my couch. Should have said go ahead and fucking fire me. I need two hundred grand and I know you got it. See what fucking happens. I don't want to sue but then if I get some press.

Blow it up to a federal case. If I could get one of the lawyers who reads my shit. Latch on to Cernovich, take it up to Ruth Bader Motherfucking Ginsburg. She'll read what I said about her dry elderly twat and I'll lose.

I did the right thing. Didn't I? Not walking off my job. Which means I get to have a shitty day every day for a very long time. Did the right thing not killing my neighbors' dog. Get to have it wake me up barking after it killed my cat. Have the neighbors who inherited money sit there in happy inherited lives in their house clad in black artisanal charred cedar. Did the right thing, pulled out in the Philippines. My unselfish genes will die. I'll die alone. Still broke. Afraid of my demented 120 year old landlady who can raise my rent up and up in the midst of the *rent crisis*. Suck out in weeks what it took me years to make. I'm powerless. Not in the good sense of *we admitted we were powerless*. Powerless over anyone who wants to take anything from me and I'll just smile and fucking take it. Won't I. This book is fictional. I don't exist.

The Gift

On her 12th birthday her mother gave her a red envelope from the mail. The family was poor. The father a drunk. The kids beat her up at school. The envelope had no return address. The upper left hand corner just said:

A GIFT

Well open it, said her mother. And she did.

It was a check for one million dollars.

In the memo section it said "You'll Never Want Again."

The address section had no name. It just said TREEHOUSE CORPORATION.

It's a prank, said the mother. Throw it away.

Yes, the girl agreed. A prank. But it's funny. I like it. I'll put it in a frame.

That's ridiculous, the mother said. Why torture yourself like that.

It's fine, said the girl. It's funny.

The next day she skipped school and rode her bike to the bank. Presented the check. I think this is a joke, she said. But can you check to be sure. The teller gave a half smile and went to get the manager. She took the check with her. The girl's heart picked up. There was a long moment at the window. The radio was playing Fleetwood Mac. *Well there you go again-- you say you want your freedom.* The manager came to the window. He wore

a light purple shirt and a dark purple tie. He was holding the check. Are your parents outside, he asked.

No, she said. I rode my bike.

I'm going to need a parent or guardian for this situation, he said.

It was real.

**

Her parents didn't steal the money. They bought a modest house. She went to a new school. They didn't beat her up there. She read French. She played viola. Before the school she didn't know what a viola was. She loved it.

She looked for TREEHOUSE CORPORATION every day at first. Then every week. Every month, every year. But she never forgot. She went to college. Majored in journalism. Asked her professors: how could you find someone from their bank account. Treehouse Corporation was an LLC owned by an S Corp owned by another LLC in Bermuda, and so on. They didn't want to be found.

She placed little classified ads. Places where someone who owned a corporation would read it. The Financial Times. The Economist. I'm the girl from Oak Grove. You gave me a gift. It changed my life. I'd like to talk to you. Please write to me.

No one did.

She got a job at a newspaper. The Paris bureau. A girl from her town, her home. She met a man, a painter. They married in June. A boy. She would speak at night about the gift. Treehouse. Let

it go, he told her. His palm on the back of her neck, kissing her hair. Let it go. It gave you a life that brought us together. It did its work. It doesn't matter anymore.

And one day there it was. In her very own paper.

A billionaire was dying. He'd built half the homes in America. He never gave interviews but now just once. He grew up poor. The father a drunk, he beat the boy. One day a kindly neighbor gave him a gift. His first ten dollars. He bought lumber. Taught himself to build. Made a place he could be safe. A treehouse.

He had no office anymore. His mysterious foundations didn't return her calls. Marcel took the baby while she flew 20 hours. Back roads to the mansion outside Omaha. She came to the gate with the high beams from the rental car cutting into cold pouring rain just as night fell. Big black button on the old intercom. Hello, she said. Hello—do you remember me. You gave me a gift.

No one answered.

Please, she said. Please—I've looked for you all my life. The cold rain fell and fell. She was crying.

And a voice came.

I can't believe you've found me, a man said. Raspy and tired like waking up from a long sleep. Is there anything you'd like to tell me. And she said: can I have some more money.

What You're Up Against

I'm sorry but I have to leave early, she tells me. Client in Ventura.

The old man sends a car. When she gets there he prepares a bath with candles. She bathes alone. He busies himself. Sneaks peeks but mostly leaves her be. When she gets out he'll massage her for a long time. Fleetwood Mac on his fancy stereo. Take her to dinner. Nicest place in town. A glass of wine at home and the car takes her back to L.A. Thousand dollars in her account.

They don't fuck. Don't even kiss. He's just lonely.

She met him on Tinder, too.

Morning Meditation

In the mood to hang myself today. To counteract this I'm in the park. To meditate. Conscious contact with my higher power. His voice is in the birds. But somewhere there's a city crew using a gas powered weed cutter or some shit. Clearing brush at 8am on a Sunday. Definitely the best time to have loud machines. Not between 9 and 5 on a weekday when people are at school and work. 8AM Sunday when the crew can make double time and people want to sleep in. Weed whacker grinding up nests full of baby birds that would have grown up to sing.

Also some Mexican event going on. *Sabado Gigante* announcer barking into the loudest PA mankind ever built. Subwoofers the size of the pyramids. State sponsored festival for childhood diabetes. You get pamphlets and a free tote bag that says Law Offices of Larry H. Parker. Lines for this extending back into the canyons. A bouncy castle, the delighted screams of children. Ice cream truck with hand drawn unlicensed Spiderman on the side, playing "Music Box Dancer." One of the teeth in the music box is broken; it's been missing a note for ten years.

So much for meditation. The weed whacker groans on. Biggest drought in history. There are no weeds. The park is pure dirt. Cactuses are wilting. But the crew has to come out. My higher power speaks. The meaning of life is: you just have to GGGRROOWORROWRROOOWRRRR

I have a date today. It won't go well. She's Asian and 33 years old. She'll be on hormonal birth control. She won't like me. She'll ask what do you do. I'm a fucking secretary. Like Maggie Gyllenhaal in the movie. I'm a pathetic piece of shit is what I

do, and my nose is broken. What do you do what do you do what do you do, they all want to know. Plus, Asians are overvalued. Every dork wants one.

I went out with another writer. She didn't like me either. Fine. She's Japanese but she looks like a Mexican with Downs syndrome. Her work. I haven't seen it but I know it's garbage. Professional fashion blogger. There's not one good fashion blogger on this planet. There's exactly one good blogger of any kind on this planet. What luck, it's me. She's an aging untalented twat with a potato sitting on top of her neck and I lost out on a third date with her to some lawyer. What does that make me.

What can I offer a woman. I don't know anything except how to write honestly. But I'm the only person who knows this. It isn't hard. Do you want it? She didn't. She wants some dork with money.

What did you expect. She's 30. At 28 women start calling men by their jobs. A hot girl who writes me from Texas joined Tinder. She goes on two dates a night. They're the surgeon, the trial lawyer, the CEO. Then she's surprised when they text her how they want to give her a house covered in rose petals. You either fuck all the time or not at all. You're either a pure pussy wizard or a sexless bumbling dork. Anyone with the monomania for a prestige job: the latter.

Still. At 28 girls chase the surgeon, the CEO. At 22 the black tar smoking bass player. Pussy chases extremes. The middle is death. A job that doesn't eat your life, art as a hobby: death. Pussy wants a mansion or pussy wants to sleep on the sidewalk. I have an apartment.

My date will flake. After I leave my house to meet her. Something came up. She won't suggest an alternate time. I'm good about not saying "cunt." Not good about holding back from turning that flash of hatred on myself. What I wanted to make me happy will make me miserable. Every god damn thing I try is an appointment in Samarra. I'll never get laid. Never get married. Never have children. Fine. Listen to me. Why would I make another one of whatever I am.

**

All right. I meditated. Of course the work crew is from the storm yesterday. Lightning hit the palms. Set them on fire. Magnificent. At night the coyotes came. Crying at each other behind the house. When I hear them I go chase them. There's always a scout. He runs just far enough to look back and know I can't catch him. Their burrow must have flooded. They're going all *Watership Down* looking for a new place to live. If they catch you, they will kill you, prince with a thousand enemies. One of these days the scout will draw me into the pack. They'll catch me and I'll have to hand it to them. What a way to go.

The PA is coming from the stadium. Some kind of youth baseball. Good for them. My date will flake or she won't and if she does it's a blessing. I know from her texts she's not my future wife. Who cares. I'll be a secretary for another fifteen years. Go to the third world. Buy an illiterate teen slave. With my first world economic power she'll be forced to squeeze out my babies and clean my toilet. Finally I'll be happy. Look at that. Spiritual progress.

God/ Pony Fucking/ Jungle Slave Wife/ Gay Teen Meth Whore

I'm not maintaining conscious contact with my higher power these days. I get it for a minute. In the morning when I go look at trees and grass. Hear the birds. In nature I remember: I'm a tiny mote in God's creation. No more significant than an insect. But no less perfect.

Can't seem to keep this in my head, out in the world. Since my dad died and I turned 40 (and also before, forever) I'm obsessed with dying childless. Being broke. Being a bad writer. Inadequate. I think I'm running the show. Blowing it harder than I could have ever imagined.

Constantly agitated. AA sponsor will tell me the solution is: more prayer. More talking to newcomers. More General Service Area Assembly Meetings, Area Committee Meetings, District Committee Meetings– have some pussy show up to just one of these fucking things just once, or back up a truck with a bomb in it.

You need to keep adding new shit. You build a tolerance to sobriety. To prayer. God, I offer myself to thee… please remove my character defects… Lord, make me a channel of thy peace… all meaningless now.

Meditation still works. Don't know what I'm communicating with. Does God exist. Who cares. The universe as this vast incomprehensible thing is enough. I'm a bacterium with a simple job. Experience the world with my senses. Eat sleep fuck shit die. Try to help other living creatures.

It comes and goes. It's better than it was. Used to believe that either a) God did not exist; anyone who believed was an idiot, or b) God existed and created the world solely to torture me. Now the prayers mean nothing, except one of the character defects will catch. I'll think of it later in the day and not fuck up. Look up mumbling Lord make me a channel of thy peace and see trees tossing in the wind. Remember something. Everything is OK and be good to people. Just do your best. Doesn't have to be better than anyone else.

**

Too tempting to look at stupid shit on the internet. You've already blown it. Go ahead and look. Twitter. That one horse porn video. Brazilian chick with a cute ass in black Speedo bikini bottoms. *Farewell to Ponny,* it's called. You could watch Ingmar Bergman films for free online probably but *Farewell to Ponny*, infinitely more compelling. You still haven't found the one. Where the horse gives a girl a visible vaginal creampie. You want to see horsecock pulsating and its 18 gallon load hosed within a human twat, but just barely so you can see the force of the liquid spewing out. You need to believe a centaur could be created.

There's no perfect horse porn. Yet *Farewell to Ponny* has an emotional throughline. Girl loves her pony. They must part. She's young, cute– most of the women in horse porn, over 30. Useless.

**

Online dating is dead. I'll have to go talk to people. Jesus Christ, I'd rather lay my summer ball sac over a severe tire damage

strip and have a parade of tractors drive over it. There are no women anywhere. What ones there are– they'd rather lay their cuntflaps over the severe tire damage strip than speak to me. Look at me.

Get out there and sell yourself. Fuck you, I'm not doing that. I'm leaving. To the jungle, where people are so poor they have to pretend to like me. Where the natives beat their women. Knock them up at fifteen and leave. They grow up in cinder block huts drinking sewer water so my four walls and TV and Brita pitcher: wealth of the pharaohs. Yes I'm exploiting people. But I'm Ward god damn Cleaver after the trike driver who blasts in her and then runs away to another island when he hears about the blessed event.

I'm sick of this shit requiring effort. I already have a job. It should just be part of nature. The world should give you pussy. I need a homeless woman whose options are me or fuck a pony. Our spoiled rotten women, with their equality and voting and their birth control and not getting hit. Fuck all that. I mean, I support it politically. But there will be no next generation because no one wants to wash the fucking dishes. I get it. I don't either.

**

Supposed to help my friend rescue her homeless teen son today. He lives in a car with two other underage gays and smokes meth. What the fuck will I tell him. Hey man– move back home and wash dishes and go to school. Read boring shit, do boring math, apply to a boring college. Get a boring job so you can boost a stock some rich douche will inherit and pump taxes into drones that set children on fire. Fuck that. Stay in the car. Smoke

your meth. Fuck for money. Save a seat for me. I can't take this fucking shit anymore.

Cry All You Want

Monday

Booze stopped making me feel good. Coke stopped making me feel good. Instead I have to work this absurd L. Ron Hubbard program where I'm a better brother friend and neighbor. Organize pancake breakfasts. Counsel at risk teens who I secretly want to fuck or beat up. Be of service to my boss and a ray of sunshine to my colleagues. I'm becoming a good person and it makes me sick. A pathetic substitute for the real happiness of being half in the bag, blowing fat chunky rails and yammering all night about my page views in Congo to some dumb pimply Amber Rose looking cunt from the downtown Standard pool.

**

Tuesday

Poor people are happier than me because they can impregnate multiple women and beat their wives. People in the Philippines who live in sewers are happier because they can fucking *give up*. There's no way you'll ever have money there. They got that system from the Spanish where two guys in suits own all the land. They just flog the other sixty million people for not picking sugar fast enough while their wives get plastic surgery. It's a curse to have opportunity. You're haunted by this idea that if you just work a little harder you might make it. If you could just grind out 1% more. That dream is a tool to keep you alive in the crab bucket. Crank up a stock owned by someone who fucking inherited it. You will never have enough money to just

fucking relax. But they make you believe you might. The thing they do in hell is make you think you might get out.

**

Wednesday

I need kids. I'll impregnate the next girl who fucks me. Just like I took the first job offer when unemployment ran out. Some lucky Tinder date. She'll have an abortion probably. But maybe not. I'll talk her out of it. Or I won't; I'll come to my senses.

Anyway the next one is getting it. I never use condoms and they never use birth control. Sometimes they ask me to strap up. Usually not, but the last one did. So I grudgingly put one on. Pantomimed fucking her with it. Then got hard again laying on top of her rubbing my tip on her pussy until she got wet enough and fucked her bare. There was a moment she gave up. Was it because she was hot enough, or was she just tired of fighting. Will you cum in my mouth, she said. Maybe she was afraid I'd cum in her. Or maybe she likes it in the mouth, who knows. Maybe I'm being too hard on myself and fucking me isn't such a disaster. Sex with me is not always rape. Maybe she just got horny. And just because I made her horny doesn't mean I'm a rapist. I'm preoccupied with rape from reading the internet too much. 75% of online writing is about rape. I think if a girl once said no in 1989 and I fucked her last week it's rape. A yes can be withdrawn at any time. A no is forever. So if she says, when we're getting out of her car to walk back through the park with the owls and into my apartment, if she says: I don't want to sleep with you, which everyone who has ever slept with me has said, and then if I make out with her with her back against the pine tree and then eat her pussy on the bed and get it in– I'm a

rapist. I'm a rapist because I took actions that made her horny enough to want to fuck me. No one could ever just want me. No one could ever be lying in the beginning. Being coy. The bedrock principle is: no woman ever wants to fuck me. Whenever I've done it it's been a trick, or rape. Anyway I want to have kids now. Otherwise life has no meaning.

**

Thursday

Angela is crazy and she needs a good beating. She got her period. Thank God, she texts. I've never been happier to see bloody sheets. The idea of having your baby makes me sick. She needs a good beating and to go in the red tent and do whatever they do in there. Complain. She broke my wall length mirror. She drove my car in the FasTrak lane and I got mailed a ticket. I managed not to spend too much money on her to feed her money/ ego/ exploit men trap but now the taxes are coming due. I managed not beat her up but she managed to get plastered in my house without me and fall into the largest piece of glass she could find. I held back but she walked out with contusions all over her ribs, neck and collarbones anyway. The end was foreordained.

**

Friday

I have a date. I know she reads my web site so I better post something deep and moving and magnificent so she immediately drops her panties. But who cares. I should start fucking whores but I'm too cheap. I should go out to San

Bernardino where Greg keeps an apartment full of coke sniffing porn actresses but it's a drive. I'd need it to plan it. Sex is an impulse. Setting it up in advance, like buying a 5 year CD to have pay for an eight ball. I need pussy to just appear.

**

Saturday

God is some eldritch transdimensional alien mouth whose food is your suffering. I should have been born in France where people work two hours a week and spend the rest of the time leering at smelly French ass in the copy room. Lingering over meals; rhapsodizing over shaved carrots.

**

Sunday

Felt a little better after AA last night. This girl Janet, a giant Jewess who shared about her advertising career. Her company contractually committed to unlimited lower thirds. The work is too much and she fears losing it. Her identity as a perfect person. She makes online ads. Terrified to lose getting paid nothing to make things everyone hates. When someone else is suffering I'm happy. God bless her though; she has kind eyes and wears tiny skirts where when the moon is right you can see all the way up to her cunt crack. Big strong thighs. Maybe I'll pop one off to her later. Her dark Jewy mein. I'll beat off to her having a hairy taint and asshole, though of course she's the type to wax.

That's all it would take not to be sick to death of AA meetings. More girls. More girls under 35, at an attractiveness level of 5.00000001 or above. And my standards, however low you think they are– lower than that. Girls who dress up, like her. Although why would they. The AA men, and me, disgusting jowly old scumbags. Every AA guy looks like they've had skin grafts over 90% of their face and the donor was an avocado.

Will the Weekend Be Wasted

Will the weekend be wasted. I could go out with— what the fuck is her name again. Colleen. First date since Bud died. It'd be a waste. Before I sleep with a man I make him show me test results, she says. It happens that I carry negative STD papers in my briefcase. But they're from October. Who have I fucked since then. Angela. Kerry who I choked. Someone else, some other Tinder Asian. But maybe not. Angela existing has relieved my need for women. We text 200 times a day. Me existing hasn't stopped her from fucking every man in Texas. What can you do.

Anyway Colleen makes you show paperwork. Even then she makes you wear a condom. Says she's never fucked without one. After the bar we made out in the back of the Subaru. I got her pants off. Very tough in the confines. Women, please wear a skirt. She's— not quite a radical feminist. But she supports Clinton for identitarian reasons. She has armpit hair and a thick copper bush as a political statement. She's over 30 but her cunt after making out at the bar, fingerfucking in the back seat— the best pussy juice in history. No men's germs have sullied her biome.

For us to have a future I'd have to believe her condom thing is bullshit. I'd have to be the guy who gets her hot eating pussy. Slip it in raw and ruin her. I'm never wearing a condom again, ever. She's terrified of STDs because she's a germ freak. Because her gay friend has HIV. Heresy to admit that gays get AIDS because they fuck a thousand strange men in toilets, huge black dongs rasping bloody shitty assholes dry. That's where AIDS comes from. Middle class Caucasian with a 401(k) ought to worry more about birth at 40. Your kid having autism. The

Zika virus of the rich. I will say she has giant Irish milk jugs. I could palpate her jiggling white tits all night. I forget if they have those blue veins that big white girl titties get. But there are freckles. After five Koreans and a Mexican you want that boiled ham.

Maybe I could pull it off. But who am I now. I respect other people's wishes. I respect women, which means we'll never speak again. Too bad. I like her.

Who am I now. Am I someone who kills his neighbors' dog. Meatball over the fence with some nice window glass in it. It's a wood fence, find a gap in the slats. Get a stick nice and sharp. The dog attacks the stick and I just jam it hard into the back of its mouth. His ruined red throat. I want to smash out all his teeth. Get the axe, take its back legs. I want to do it in front of their kid. Maybe wait till he's old enough to form memories.

Who am I now. Not someone who kills the neighbors' dog. I'm someone who lets the neighbors' dog kill my cat and I just take it, I guess. My sponsor talked me out of reporting it to animal control. Strike one is nothing. Strike two: city kills the dog. I knew I would take no revenge, when Bud died. I had a feeling that felt like it came from God. Let there be no more suffering from this. They're nice people. They'll keep their fucking dog inside.

I don't want another animal to die. Someone else's pet, because of this thing that was an accident. But it's an accident because a pit bull can't make decisions. It can't make decisions because it's a killing machine. Killing is its job. Being your pet is its hobby. He knew he did something bad, they said. I wanted them to know I'd do something bad. In a week that dog will be gone,

I wanted to tell the guy. How it goes down is up to you. I want to cut up their kid in front of the dog. Who am I now.

The cat's gone. Scattered his ashes. Pair of mourning doves moved into the yard a day later, in the space where he sat. I come close. They're not afraid of me. Some part of them knows.

The Fleas

The god damn fleas are killing me. Have to do work to take care of it. Fine. This is an opportunity. Clean the house. Take care of yourself– no. Fuck this, fuck all of this, fuck the Earth. We need more terrorism, more war. More Nazis, more racism, more mass rapes, more child slavery. More school shootings more North Korean nukes. Can something fucking good happen today please. It won't. You have to make your own luck. What a pain in the ass.

My cat died. His fleas have had ten generations to develop into fiends that crave human flesh. Crawl under the blankets half dead at night and there's tickling in my leg hairs. Look under the sheets with my iPhone flashlight. Dozens of them feasting on the fat blue veins snaking around my ankle bones.

I looked them up. They're hard to kill. Why is every other organism so superior. I could die from tripping on a tree root. Fleas can lay dormant for 50 years. They wake up, fuck once, impregnate a flea woman with 1,000 more fleas. Fleas can jump the equivalent of 300 yards. Fleas' exoskeletons, like 3 inch steel plate. Fleas have 9 inch cocks. They turn into men at night and ruin your girl's pussy. Fleas have small noses and 10,000 Tinder matches. Fleas all have book deals. 30,000 twitter followers. Fleas are luminaries in "alt" literary movements and have appeared in the New Yorker. Fleas sit in back of your AA meeting with the one hot girl you spotted three weeks ago and thought you had a shot with. The only sober Asian under 30. The flea looks like John F. Kennedy and you're an uglier James Cromwell. Fleas have bought and held Vangaurd ETFs since age 25 and have no terror of retirement. Fleas flirt with the barista effortlessly and she makes an effort back and forgets the

1,000 scintillating times you ordered cocoa. Fleas can squat past parallel without their leg bones creaking like they're about to have Joe Theisman's compound fracture. Which was from a flea flicker.

They get on my computer at night. Leave nasty Amazon reviews. Comments on my web site. Punch up your writing more, they tell me. Listen faggot– you go write some shit. You could practice for a thousand years and never approach what I pull out of my ass. From now on one comment is allowed: *I'm a woman, fuck me*. I look forward to your feedback.

Where the fuck are my spiders now. My cereal box is full of silverfish. Back of the toilet aswarm with house centipedes. They do jack shit. They don't eat a single flea. Just their own mates and young. My predatory arthropods: fucking bums. Like having a lion infestation, still being constantly gored by wildebeest.

Women Recently

Now I'm thinking about her while she's not thinking about me. Has not ever thought about me. She's thinking about video shoots that guys from bands invited her to, while I'm thinking about her. Cool interesting people are inviting her to swimming pools. I'm buying unnecessary trash bags at Target to get out of the house.

**

I should take a year off. Not write. Nothing good comes. What does doesn't make me famous. Only pussy I'm getting is return traffic. No new girls find me, since I stopped being a misogynist.

Meanwhile I have a bug bite on my right calf that I'm convinced is from this fat chick with the fried out green hair who I fucked Sunday, just to fuck somebody. She did have perfect tits. She did have an IUD, so I could blast in her, her laying on her stomach, one of my legs between her legs. Big tits and perfect small nipples. That's something. I also liked her gut. It wasn't doughy. Wall of muscle behind it. What if someone appraised you this way. As long as she fucked me who cares.

Anyway she gave me bedbugs. Does permethrin take care of bedbugs too. Probably not. Probably I'll be gnawed on by bedbugs forever. Plus the fleas re-awakening. I didn't thoroughly vacuum my home every day for 7 months per the permethrin can. Just spray once, it says. Then just spend a week's pay on an industrial vacuum, decibels like a fighter jet engine with your head stuck in the turbine. Crank the weight of this rickety thing around for hours in the heat every day forever,

is all you have to do. It stimulates the eggs to hatch. Fuck it. Welcome back fleas. We've endured.

**

She had a bad sunburn and she was drunk, but stroking her ass while she bent over to look at my computer screen. Her pussy. Almost wanting to cum as soon as I put it in. Her on top moving fast with my legs pressed close together. Slow doggystyle. I wanted to really feel it. My load was one thick shot almost to the back of her neck. Then one halfway up her back. Then like an eight minute wait for the rest of it. My dick shaking like it was choking on a chicken bone while crickets literally chirped out the window. I asked if I could cum in her. How good is your insurance, she said.

**

Lara wouldn't fuck me again. She thinks if we don't she wins. Instead we watched Game of Thrones. Spent too much money on sushi and I'd feel a lot better if the night ended with a fuck. But maybe I'll never get laid again. I need Lara because I need an Asian. The specific Japanese porno muff with long thick pointy hairs splaying straight out of fat dark pussylips taint and asshole.

**

Tonight is my second date with what the fuck is her name. Rebecca. She takes Zoloft and Wellbutrin. Zoloft is the "primary," she says, and the Wellbutrin is so she can cum. Hairy pussy and an IUD. Big perfect tits with tiny perfect nipples like mine. We have identical nipples. Never thought to be grateful

for my nipples before. But I've been catching girls lately with eight square feet of nipple meat. Each areola bump should be a nipple of its own. She's married.

I love a soft belly but too many pigs lately. Now I need to fuck a gymnast built like a little boy. Suck on little nonexistent tits with pecs under them. Tiny lean muscular panther ass. Fucking a fat girl can make you doubt yourself. She's a human being, you don't want to think these things. But you do. You can nut in her while she's ovulating. I like the smell of her cunt– which I couldn't find at first. I kept feeling this spongey yet hard meat button. Discovered it was her asshole. How did I not know this.

**

Who am I forgetting. Holly from AA who wanted me to rape her in some dork's apartment she was house sitting. None of them feel like anything. None of them count. A girl's wonderful and then she's nothing. Drugs are wonderful, booze wonderful, money probably wonderful but I wouldn't fucking know. Food shelter air and drinking water all fucking great until they aren't anymore. You're built to suffer. Your big brain which you think is to make tools, fight off rampaging ground sloths– it's to trick another man out of pussy until he brains you with a rock with his finely honed Darwinian hands. It's to take things away from other people. Them or you. Money food pussy. We're innately evil. We deserve suffering.

I want Anna back but she won't speak to me. Her sister had a manic episode. Crashed her car in flames on the freeway. Lost her job. Fell in with dirtbags. Anna has to babysit her. I don't talk to her about the crash, she says. Too delicate. I try to keep

her mind on other things. Otherwise it could set her off. She'll harm herself.

The sister picked up Anna's phone and called me. Something something motherfucker don't ever text my sister about me again. Please calm down, I said. Just listen to yourself. She said well motherfucker I'm not going to listen to *you*...

I told her: go get in another flaming car wreck, cunt. Go smoke crack and get gang banged by methheads again you whore. When I stopped she kept going. Something something I know where you work. I said that's right, I have a job. I didn't get fired for being crazy like you, you useless piece of shit.

One of us hung up. Now Anna won't talk to me. I'm afraid the sister will kill herself. But suddenly I can laugh again.

Destroy the Earth

If my sister reads your post she'll try to get you fired, she says. Even with the fake name. She gets vengeful about this sort of thing.

Well what can you do. What I said is true. So I said it. Maybe someone will get me fired. Maybe I should have started anonymous. Not shown anyone my shit. Not put up Youtube videos of my face for radio and voice for silent film. But: some people find me to fire me. Some people find me to fuck me. I want to get fucked more than I don't want to get fired.

I have a zero drag lifestyle. An unmarried childless drone who rents. No girlfriend, no serious prospect for a girlfriend, no serious prospect for having a serious prospect for a girlfriend, ever. I'm 40. Every male relative dies at 67 from cancer. Before that their minds slip from chemo. Maybe 15 years left of being sharp, if you can call this sharp. My hips are going. My eyes. My hair going white and I have the ball sac of a 120 year old man. You can't beat me. I've already lost. If your sister gets me fired I'll stand by the banks of the river, and wait.

Part of me would welcome being doxxed. Fired. The greatest job I've ever had still sucks. Allows me material possessions I don't fucking need. I could pack all this shit in a pit and toss a match on it and go sleep on the ground somewhere and laugh. Life leaving me. Time speeds up. Days upon days I don't remember. Getting old; it's already over, I do not fucking care what happens as long as it's not a maiming or prison– anything that takes my freedom. A great job– I make enough that I pay enough taxes to support another one of me. He's in a Section 8 studio up in the Hotel Cecil. Some haunted spot downtown

where they find suicides in the rooftop water tank. Disability checks cashed into Steel Reserve the instant they arrive. I pray that that's where the money goes. The other me. The happier one. Find me. Fire me. I do not fucking care.

Last thing I was living for was my cat. The neighbor's pit bull shook him to death. No reason I can't leave except being scared about retirement money. So I can retire with no memories of a good life; I spent the whole god damn time working. Worked like a dog since I was fucking fourteen. I'll die alone, slowly, in the worst way imaginable. That is a certainty.

I hate this city. I hate it in my bones because of the women. Not one good woman in LA. Probably not one in America. They live to abuse you. They live to make you dance. Then they have the sheer balls to accuse you of entitlement.

Or: I love the land but hate its people. Great birds here but my rent is over sixteen grand a year for a stucco building. Cinder block walls around the parking lot. Family of three upstairs playing tympani on the pergo floors at 3AM– and that's a *steal*. My landlady has dementia. She'll die and the place will be bought up in aggregate by Berkshire Hathaway. Rent will instantly blow up to *market rate,* which is to say 88% of median household income. Increased cost of living makes money meaningless, always. There is always *market efficiency.* I. e. whatever you have they'll take– the Rothschilds, the Waltons, the reptilians, whatever you call them– *they.* The inherited money people. The interest of the interest of four hundred years of slave ship money people absolutely *will* extract any inefficiency aka money freedom happiness.

Destroy my job, destroy society, destroy the planet. I have nothing to lose. I am connected to nothing. Find me fuck me fire me– fucking *free* me.

I have a 401K. It did not go up with good news in the stock market. It will go down with Brexit. Because of course. When oil prices rise, gas prices rise the same day. When oil prices fall, gas prices take months to catch up. Of course. There's some wonky reason some second-tier ivy schlump can explain to you on CNBC. Some NPR twat who was driven to field hockey practice in a toast colored Volvo 240 wagon with a Choate Rosemary Hall sticker on it can explain over piano jazz, but any bum can tell you: *they want more money, and they can take it.* The government exists only to speed this up. The government is hideous money spergs hypnotizing fetal alcohol syndrome snake handlers. TED talk tax cheats hustling the background cast of Denny's fight videos.

If you want to predict the future, ask what makes heirs more money. What takes the masses' time, freedom, happiness. That's what will happen. We had a movement to free women. It multiplied the misery of both sexes. Women forced to work, men forced to work more when women don't want a man who doesn't have more than her. Pure evil.

What will you do if you get fired. You could write full time. No I fucking can't. You can't write and eat. Nobody reads. Every web site, every publishing house is Buzzfeed. Liars forever chasing shrinking money. The whole culture, sweatshops of pure shit run by reptilians for aspiring reptilians. I'll clean toilets.

Someone may get me fired. I may or may not fuck them up. But I'll for sure make them think I *might*. Every minute of the shoe not dropping another minute I could be prepping to hurt them bad. Really I'll be beating off. I won't say to who. She's the type to get revenge.

Pussy is the Only Thing

As I was washing shit off my dick with the citrus almond hand soap I tried to feel bad. I couldn't. I tried to be afraid of HIV; scrutinized my shiny white shaft under the surgical bathroom light for blood. Raw anal sex with runaway meth hookers: frowned upon by the CDC. But I was intact. What's more, the transmission rate for the– what's the opposite of the "receptive partner"– the guy who puts his dick in never gets it. I tried to think about hanging myself like I have at least ten times a day for a month. Couldn't. I tried to picture my dead dad, my dead friend, my dead cat looking down on me from heaven. Shaking their heads at the boy they loved doing self destructive shit. Their ghosts were gone. I was just there in the downstairs shower getting hard again, thinking about eight minutes ago.

I'd been to a therapist. My AA sponsor told me to go. He's obsessed with getting me over my sex shit now that I've not had a drink for two years. Now that I'm a lawn cutting bill paying ordinary taxpayer with a certified pre owned family sedan. Now that my credit rating inches toward normalcy. Now that I talk to my family. Help newly sober dorks. Grit my teeth and tell them how fucking great everything is, now that I've done my step work and surrendered control to my higher power. I'm achieving my dreams. Do you know that my second book is out. People like it; it's not bad I gather but I have no fucking idea anymore. Looking at it one more time is a bridge too far. Anyway I've got my act together so it's time to stop doing the one thing that brings me happiness. Raw sex with young girls.

She's nineteen. Her parents are Jehovah's witnesses, of course. The people who knock on your door in suits on a hot Saturday and ask: have you thought about eternity– their daughters will

all smoke meth in a San Bernardino County squat. Their sons will build underground porno vaults with 8mm clips of children fucked by raccoons and tortured to death. I'll say this: she's spiritual.

Where was I– I was at the therapist to work on relationship issues. With my gold PPO insurance I have this luxury. There were Frank Lloyd Wright chairs in the waiting room. In the office, a tall Pottery Barn water feature. My sponsor told me to go because I want to get married and have kids. He thinks as long as I fuck Tinder whores it'll never happen. I think if I stop fucking Tinder whores and meet my future wife she'll look at me like dog shit. I think women only respect you if you're already fucking someone hotter, and you treat them like garbage. I'm right.

I also think I'll never meet my future wife. I think if I signed up for a cupcake baking class like people say it'd be ten lonely dudes, two ugly girls. I think if I don't work agonizingly for pussy every day nothing happens. Most times not even then. If I work for it it's not love. I'll never get my princess moment, is what I'm saying. But I did once. I fell in love with a girl from work. Now she's dead. Everything circles back to my dad my ex my cat and how I'll die alone. Until today.

I let the therapist have it. Everything in 50 minutes. It helps to write it up for four years, then cut it down and down to where you have every canned metaphor memorized. Great for AA shares too. People come up after meetings and ask are you a writer. I say no. I want them to feel less talented than some schlump off the street, because I resent their TV jobs.

I told him I want to hang myself. That I think my mom will get cancer. That I'll get cancer. I'll get fired and be broke or I'll never get fired and have to work forever. Never have kids. Die alone. I write; I used to like it but now I hate it from looking at it. I made a book so new people could see my shit but I had to go on fucking Twitter to sell it. Sales still terrible and looking at twitter to sell the book sucked me into our culture: I hate women I hate men I hate blacks whites cops. *As a Black Man, Pokemon Go asks me to put my life in danger* says Kotaku. Corporate pop culture plus corporate social justice, over and over. I worked in Hollywood when *Cowboys and Aliens* was about to come out. They thought it would be big. You'd have to sit in meetings with a big grid trying to come up with movies like *Cowboys and Aliens*. Knights, dinosaurs, robots on one side. Werewolves, vampires, Godzilla on the other. That's what Kotaku is, and everything else. Just bankrupt.

Kotaku is a multimillion dollar web site. Hacks get paid and don't have to work. I'm honest and do my best; I sell close to zero books and if anyone finds out about my writing I'll get fired. There's that trivial garbage rabbit hole but also I'm afraid I'll hang myself. Afraid my best friend will hang himself. More people will die and I'll be alone. Angela will leave me or I'll hurt Angela. I'm afraid of hurting her with this post. I'm afraid and I'm going to die and nothing I do can help. Well our time is up, he said.

Got out and El Chuco called saying he'd left his car in Rosemead. Could I help him get it. It's a Tesla. God knows where he got the money but you can open it with your phone. I unplugged it from the back of the Days Inn hooker hotel. Drove it at 110 out to the brothel he keeps in Redlands, now that his wife left him. The idea was one of the girls would take a picture

reading my book naked. I'd post it on twitter. Sales would result. He said send a picture with your shirt off so I can get the girls hot.

I wasn't going to fuck anyone because I Don't Do That Anymore. But I showed up and she was cute. She was bent over snorting an eight inch rail of coke off a rose gold Macbrook pro and I laid my cock between her ass cheeks and stroked her back, slipped a finger in her, picked her up and put her on the granite kitchen island counter after moving the pickle jar. She could move. We switched to the futon. She got on top and I had to tell her slow down I'm gonna cum too fast. The whole thing's on video. Except the part where I look ripped picking her up.

Upstairs in her room she had a plate of coke, hash, crushed up oxy's, xanax and molly. I'll say this for AA: I didn't think about touching it. Big shard of meth sitting on the Bank of America folder that had the mortgage papers for the house in it. Perfect hex crystal like a display at the natural history museum. If you want nineteen year old girls in your house, get drugs.

Later I was in the hot tub and she came out naked. How did you get over your sickness she asked. I read your book. You were crazy. Now you seem OK. How did you do it. When did it happen. Messengers from God everywhere. She sat on my lap and talked about trying to figure out her place in the world. Sang me a nice song while I just looked at her. She was perfect. I just want to touch you so I can remember you, I told her. You won't, she said.

At night she led me back to her room and kissed me and my mouth went numb. She got on top of me and moved. Put me in her asshole and I just liked looking at it. As soon as she got

going I sprayed a corn silo full of goo into her sigmoid. I said goodbye. Cleaned off. Ubered to my car. Drove home, got on livechat with Amazon.com to complain about a package.

Now this morning. I have a reflex to go to that dark place where I want to die. I can't get there. It just stops. The sun's out and the trees hiss in the wind and I want to live, go to dinner with my mom later. Drugs didn't work. Therapy doesn't work. Money, service, friends, family don't work. This works. I'll never stop.

Therapy Is Working

How about some positivity. Therapy's working. Two sessions, we got to blaming my parents. I have homework, to think about how my parents fucked me up. This morning I conceived of them as ordinary people. It made me sick. I'm like them. Lower middle class tax payer. Throwaway sentence in the history books, in aggregate with other schlumps. *The smallfolk dwelled in smelly apartments, paid bills, jerked off feverishly waiting for their Family Pak of chicken to cook. Still, they found meaning in love and children. Except one guy.*

I'm one of God's perfect creatures. Here to experience beauty in the world. Moved by this I went out in public. Sat in a shady patch in the park. Every conversation around me: Pokemon. Plus there's a disturbing trend now of black men and Asian women. White men used to be their "bad boy," but they've correctly surmised that we too are weak small penis nebbishes. Fashionable Kanye looking blacks will absorb all world pussy. Even Asians, the only good kind. Pussy capitalism reaches new nadirs. 13 illuminati suck up all world capital and a thousand black Chads hoard all American pussy. So be it. All I want is a flesh robot that looks like a Japanese 14 year old. How has no one made this. They have apps for every god damn thing. I'll give her the Voigt Kampf test while reaming her. The tortoise bit will make her pussy clench.

Some positivity. I can breathe. I don't have cancer– except typing "cancer" probably gives me cancer. Well if I have cancer I don't know about it. Same as not having it.

Good haircut. When I wear my tight gay T shirt my *latissimi dorsi* ripple in a manner that would please women, if my face

were perfect and I earned at least $2.5 million a year. I have a date later. Asian; name something like "Dong." I'll run my tongue over every salty inch of Dong on my flagging mattress. Smear the smell and taste of Dong over my sweaty body. Can't stop looking at pictures of Dong. Dong penetrated me deeply. Who knows. She's enthusiastic about the date. So she'll be worse than her pics. But I will accept Dong. I'll stroke Dong rapidly until Dong convulses and pukes, et cetera.

Therapy reminded me– I need to change shit. When I got sober and found God my prayers meant something. Helping others helped me. Now prayers mean as much as the instructions on the ramen packet. I know that my help does nothing. Every addict I've reached out to has relapsed and is worse off. I saw a guy I sponsored lurking by the Coinstar machine at Vons, headphones on, waiting to scrimp lost nickels off the rack geeked out on meth. My sponsee in prison wrote me back. Said: I got paroled so I'm not going to do more work inside. He'll get out and kill people.

Shit stops working. You have to find new shit. This includes God. You must find a new God or a new way to experience God constantly. Just like you can't jerk off to the same Xhamster pussy. Or the same nationality of pussy, or the same species fucking the pussy– you can't say the same prayers and do the same kindly acts. You need a mule raping a dwarf. Even then you get sick of them all being Brazilian. Too few countries poor enough for horse fucking but rich enough for video. You have to confuse the the muscle.

Slice of Life

The toilet clogged this morning. When the landlady fixed my shower she also put some giant volume of something– concrete maybe– in the tank. So water isn't being used in each flush. She's been obsessed with this for years. First she tried a Mountain Dew 2 liter filled with seltzer, which gassed out and floated uselessly. Then a couple attempts with some kind of surgical bag full of gel.

The latest try she didn't tell me about. Just the next day I noticed the water level in my toilet was one inch over the hole going into the sewer. This week I made spaghetti. Bought a 3 pound bag of frozen blueberries. My shits, giant and sticky and black. Every morning I flush twice. First flush just fills the bowl to the bottom lip with swirling dark turds and the one insulting wad of smeared toilet paper spiraling around. The second one, where I have to turn off the water at the wall first, then flush, makes it juuuuuust up to the meniscus, menacing the bathroom floor with agitated churning chunks of stool before slowly, slowly receding down after long seconds of suspense.

This morning I tried that trick again. Shit water oozed over the side of the bowl into the crack between the tiles. Almost out to the carpet. Had to sop it up with paper towels. Open the top of my old store brand cleanser with bleach spray bottle, which won't spray anymore since a bug crawled in the nozzle. Dump the bleach on the floor. Walk in the wet spot to sterilize the parts of my bare feet that had stepped in shit water. Later I noticed bleach spots on my carpet. Like the man said: the Industrial Revolution and its consequences have been a disaster for the human race.

You Will Have Nothing That You Want

Thirsty but not thirsty enough to fuck girls ugly enough to fuck me. Supposed to write today. Won't happen. I have ideas in the shower. They vanish as I soap my asshole. I'll write nothing. Nothing for a year and that's fine. Ten years, twenty years, until I'm dead, who fucking cares. If you want something you can't have it. It's when you remove desire that things come. Actually no– if you *don't* want something you cant have it either. You just can't have anything. God is a demon who eats suffering. Our world a rich banquet.

The fish tank is too loud. I meant to meditate, take a shit while reading the finest literature– instead I looked at the *Witcher 3* subreddit. Re-read the first pages of the Unabomber manifesto.

I was in Palm Spings. My friend's wife rented a house. His 40th birthday. We sat by the pool. I'd like to complain but I had a great time. His wife's brother is a beachy Burning Man money type; he had a young girl who was fun to look at. Would have been great to have single girls there but let's not go nuts. No one will ever put a woman in a social situation with me again. I must milk internet fame and fuck girls who write me until I'm dead. I must keep posting, or mail bombs.

My friend's into politics. MSNBC was on. Every ad for a drug. When I turned 120 my pancreas didn't work the way it should, until I asked my doctor about Lumitra. Don't take Lumitra if you have a liver or kidneys. You may experience hemorrhaging. When my foot rotted off from diabetes I thought I'd never coach my granddaughter's gymnastics team again. Now there's Xynquentra. The grandchild gazes lovingly at the old drug taker

as they groom horses or play trumpet. The dream, to have a young person care you're alive.

I'd been reading about news ratings. Trump went to Mexico. Fox news led with 6 million viewers. 450,000 in the "news demo." The news demo is 25-54s, versus 18-49s that most ratings track.

The other 5.5 million, older than the stones. They've wandered the Earth 300 ages of men.

Panels discuss Trump. He's shown in a pink tie at a black church swaying awkwardly while a woman glances sideways at the camera like she expects spiders to pour out of it. MSNBC has a thing where they put the lights right in the pro-Trump panelists' eyes so they blink constantly. The liberals never blink. Trump doesn't hate Mexicans, explains a Mexican he hired.

MSNBC plays to four million vampires and the five of us in the room. We're the news demo. We discuss. For everyone else it's a given: Trump will exterminate all blacks. Push Mexicans across the border into lava. When they talk Hillary's campaign it's "we." The campaign, a referendum on Race in America. I'm in favor of Mexicans. I'll vote for Hillary. But in my heart I want Trump to win and kill all minorities because I'm mad girls don't like me.

Jesus Christ, I cant even write dumb shit anymore. I cant write anymore. Relax. We knew it would be like this. You'll never write again, accept it. You are nothing. If you masturbate you can't write. Before you masturbate you can't write. You're trapped alone but if you go be with people you'll hate them

unless they fuck you. Tinder's broken; you cant even get a fat woman to the duck pond, slip around later in her smelly loose pussy.

Anyway the news is for old people. Bernie Sanders was on. He looks great. It's too bad he still exists because you're reminded that Hillary spends her time sucking on baby brains with the Rothschilds in the Hamptons. Jerking off with a fetus leg to drone footage of Yemeni boys screaming on fire. Then a $100,000 per plate lamb entree. Did you read Garrison Keillor's Trump piece, my friend asks. So cutting. You are Queens, says Garrison Keillor who is brought to you by Mercedes Benz. I don't like Trump but I like when he makes Lady Rothschild gag.

They're both horrendous pieces of shit. Trump is a fuckin buffoon but Hillary makes me believe in lizard people. The only good news is legally the president can only kill Arabs. Shuffle money from one Rothschild to another while you work for nothing. Pay taxes so the lucky poor can fuck succulent teens while you die in a world of bills. Kazcsynski's right. Our society is garbage. America must be annihilated. In ten years would be great. Yesterday would be better. Let the Canadians eat our bones. Give the land to the Mexicans. They can't do worse. Where is my fucking candidate.

MSNBC cuts away from one of their Hootie black guys. Reporter on the beach in Jersey. A hurricane unexpectedly did not hit. He still has to stand there. He must still talk up the high winds, as an elderly woman walks by with a sun parasol. A kid builds a house of cards, another folds origami cranes. As you see Nancy it's somewhat frothy now, but just 12 hours ago these seas churned with thousand legged spiny horrors. The camera's

rolling so you must speak. But there is no story. Civilization will continue. You will have nothing that you want.

You Should Message Me If Part 4

I need a girl who's a total loser but not bad looking. Who some other guy hasn't got to first. I need a girl who has no job no car no place to live but not because they smoke crack or some shit. I need a girl who's smart but no education. Could some day be a good mother but not a girl from a good family, ever– no one who talks to her dad. None of this good college Fortune 500 shit, I need a girl who earns minimum wage at the water store but doesn't feel compelled to describe herself as CEO of me incorporated or some girly Etsy shit. Ambition makes me puke. I need a girl with no pets no friends who'll move in with me and shut the fuck up while I play the *The Witcher 3*. Not even *The Witcher 3*— I play The *Witcher 3* so my *Witcher 3* character can play *Gwent*, the game-within-a-game in *The Witcher 3*. A girl who won't talk while I'm playing *Gwent* all night. Just watch.

I need a girl with no job no car no home. Can't cook can't clean– I need a girl who can't read, can't tie her shoes, can't lift a fork to her mouth because this is the level of loser it has to be to get the other thing I need: a hot woman who's single. Not dating a musician if she's under thirty or a silver fox rich guy if she's my age. My OKCupid profile is rated so low my home screen suggestions are all fat transsexuals. Five circle pics of stubbly Fred Flintsone hog jowls with lipstick and names like gloryhole_vixen. They lie about their age.

Getting addicted to *The Witcher 3*. My eyes are yellow today. Or just bloodshot, I can't tell. Yellow eyes means yellow fever. I went to the Amazon, didn't get vaccinated. Liver failing. Really it's from smearing Curel Intensive Care on my eyelids, blinking it into my eyes. Too vain not to moisturize but too

cheap to buy eye cream. Slight headache. Little trickle of snot pus oozing ever so slightly out my left nostril and my left nostril only. It's cerebrospinal fluid. Precursor to a brain hemorrhage. I have Zika. I have cancer; it's that new freckle on my cheek or the red bumps from the sun on my nose which I'll have to get cut off. Leave a skull hole in my face; I'll have to use a cunningly crafted prosthetic. Fine. Give me one like Casper van Dien. Cancer everywhere; I'm going to die and I wasted my life working instead of buying tech stocks early and pumping pulsating cumshots into underage Southeast Asian teens all day every day.

I need a hot idiot who's on SSI but forgot to mail in the forms. It's live with me or suck dick under a bridge. Even that's a tough choice. Coming to realize I'm violently undesirable. Anyway let's fuck.

Election

At least people I hate are miserable. At least Amanda Marcotte cried. As for the bad news: this will solve nothing. This will not collapse society. There will not be mass rapes. Life will continue to get incrementally worse. It would have happened under Hillary. It will happen under Trump. Every American must be annihilated with atomic weapons. Land given back to the coyotes. It's the only solution.

I felt bad for her. Read about her too wracked with sobs to talk on the phone. Trying to tell a friend through her shuddering snot-cry that it was Comey... Comey... Too emotional for a concession speech. She had to send out Podesta, the squirelly jizz guzzling hustler who rapes babies then eats them for Satan. I felt bad. She has $300 million from telling the board of Goldman Sachs that the Rothschilds have it too hard in this world. She kills children. I wanted to hold her while she cried. Because she's a woman.

We knew she sucked. It didn't matter. She had the most money. She was inevitable.

America is a shit country. All there is to it. I've been fucked up for three weeks. I went to a doctor who told me to get a CAT scan. I have money and Cadillac insurance. The insurance left wing politicians talk about to illustrate how good rich people have it. Doesn't matter. Still have to get a referral. Wait eight weeks. What I need costs a grand. I'd gladly pay cash to be done with it. You can't. Have to be billed 28 grand so your insurance can haggle it to 3 grand of which you pay a grand. For the CAT scan to exist unnecessary millions must be poured into corporations so people can have jobs they hate. The entire

American system, a holocaust of people's lives. So five rich people can have money. It costs $68,000 a year to go to college. It costs $700,000 to buy a house. The good news is it can't last. Women don't have babies because they work. This system will die. The bad news is Trump won't speed it up. He's no different.

I dropped a barbell on my head which may have caused my skull to crack and blood to seep into my brain. Rendering me retarded and unable to– well I can still work. I just can't enjoy anything. You get the opposite head injury that you pray for. Three weeks and my head feels like someone hit it with a pipe yesterday. Might have a scab sitting on my brain slowly making me unable to remember words like… like… faggot, relax. It's nothing. I was at the gym because I must resemble *Amityville Horror* era Ryan Reynolds for a high BMI 6 at the end of reproductive usefulness to respond on Tinder. My opener is a better piece of writing than anything about Donald Trump but people who write about Trump get paid for it. You have to write about Trump or fucking Brianna Wu. I had to clean and jerk a big weight over my head because the same three guys are always on the squat rack. They powerlift. Then talk about powerlifting. A great way to work hard and still look like shit.

Trump won. That night I heard jets overhead. A man screaming in the street: what the fuck is wrong with this country. Could this be it. Echo Park has New York rent but Mexican crime and infrastructure. Once in a while the water comes out green. Once in a while a borracho picks a fight with you on the sidewalk. Little guys but all nonwhites have fast hands. There's still a drunk who stands in his front yard on Montana street and yells at white people. Hey white boy get the fuck out of my neighborhood, he says. Back when I had style they'd scream hey faggot. You know there's a country next door where you

don't have to see us, I tell him. You people ruin everything, he says. Well next time invent the wheel, stupid. Go the fuck back to Hollywood he says. Too many Mexicans, I tell him.

He did not break my windows to start the race war. Now he'll get deported. Some square like me will move in. The rent will go up.

Could this be it. Why didn't I buy that gun. Pinch a couple water cooler bottles from work. Get a 40 dollar satchel of Costco beef jerky; enough calories to take me through the ice age. Because you'd have shot yourself with the gun. You'd have got bored, opened up the beef jerky pouch. You'd be fat and the Xbox controller would smell like teriyaki.

Trump won. He ran against the banks then tried to hire Jamie Dimon. Of course. It was time to get serious. You need the A team to run a hideously complex usurious system of parasites designed to crush human lives. Suck up the lifeblood of the people and planet. The stock market went up. It goes up no matter what. That's what we are for. Quarterly gains.

Of course the Aztecs did have wheels. But they only put them on toys. For real work they had slaves to drag the rocks around, until they weren't useful. Then they got publicly hacked apart. They might have used what they had to make things easier for everyone. But then what would people have done with themselves.

Week in Review

I'm a crack smoking compulsive masturbator. Nine hours a day I have to drive a robot that dresses and talks like Mitt Romney. PPO insurance and a 401(k) but I still asked for pics from the black chick who sucked my dick off Tinder. Her at 17, pregnant by a skinhead. Twins. I need pics of your underage swollen belly to beat off to, was the third thing I said to her. I can only cum now to pregnant teens. My body knows I've failed to reproduce. No pheromonal whiff of my genes out there. My balls become desperate. Climb the walls like they're being gassed. She came through.

You Should Message Me If Part 5

I need the doorbell to ring. It's you. Come in. Wordlessly bend over and I stick it in your crusty cunt and cum before I'm halfway in because you caught me before my post work jerk. Wordlessly leave. Nine months later send a picture holding a slimy red faced worm. A note that says I don't want any money. Just wanted you to know.

Come over and power bottom me with an asshole you've meticulously purged with spring water. When I cum in 15 seconds your face turns into a screen playing *Witcher 3*. I need you to fuck me then spread your legs, open your pussy, give birth to another hotter girl who also fucks me while you clean the toilet.

Seriously though just make me not do 100% of the work 100% of the time. Be reasonably not ugly. I just need hot enough to get me hard and you'd be shocked what gets me hard. Hot enough to make me cum too fast but not so hot you can leave me too easy and move too Provence. Have your life paid for by a male model who sells extremely pure cocaine. This happened to my last ex. Something like it happened to every other ex too. Every woman I've had is a fool* but they can all pick up a rich six foot eight Frenchman with a cock like a stonehenge pillar. As soon as they get rid of me.

I want to impregnate a thirteen year old foster child. Keep her in a finished basement until she has the baby and I eat it. I want a girl like Nell kept chained up in a cabin until pubescence. Part her three cunt hairs, launch load after load into her dumb young womb. Try not to laugh at her inchoate moans. Her na na ta ta ra-ah fucking Lady Gaga lyrics. I want a robot who takes my

cum then tickles my ass while her eyes play Preston Jacobs Youtube videos. Maybe you're the next best thing.

I deserve a medal for not knocking up underage girls in the Philippines. I'm not evil so my genes will be extinguished. Didn't since I thought I'd regret it but every day regret not doing it. Should have split open every junior high aged slave, dropped full loads in every IQ 76 hut dweller. But I did the right thing. I'm still miserable. Take human kindness and blow it out your ass. If I had an ounce of courage I'd be on that plane now. Back outside the Kenny Rogers Roasters in Manila. First biological female I find, take her raw for 500 pesos. When you cum in them they ask for your Facebook. To blackmail you for water buffalo vet bills. Well the exchange rate must be better now. Thanks, Trump.

* Except you

Your Pussy Your Problem

I was up at 6AM Saturday. Two missed calls and a text time stamped midnight. *I have Astrid's phone. She said to call you. It's kind of an emergency.*

I can't get afraid girls are dead anymore. All I thought was: if you send a text like this you better explain, faggot. Some day I'll wake up to a text that she's dead. I accept this. But it better say: *Astrid is dead.* Not *can you call me it's kind of urgent.* Don't be a chick about it.

Also: your pussy your problem. If you're high with her you're fucking her. You broke it you bought it. Roll her on her stomach. I've done this 100 times. When she starts OD'ing she fights any attempt to save her life. She'll bite you. Don't be afraid to pop her one. It feels good, like you're a detective in an old movie. If you really think it's bad call 911. She'll wake up suddenly. She wants you to think she's dying but she doesn't want bills. She wants you to hit her and rape her while she's unconscious. Trust me. I met her on OKCupid too.

The problem is the other love of my life. Now dead. She'd also bite you when you rolled her over. She took too many pills one night. I couldn't wake her up. This made me mad so I went outside and kicked her car over and over. Walked home; on the way there was a beautiful ornamental tree in flower on the sidewalk. I climbed up it and ripped it in half. Ten years now I've driven by that tree, on Berendo south of Franklin. It never grew back. It's next to another specimen of the same tree that I did not rip in half, which has flourished and flowers beautifully every year. Every time I drive by I think "sorry, tree." Things don't grow back. They don't get better.

Her dying broke the theory that they just get over it. She can die from this. She will. One day I'll get the text. A matter of time. Will it happen now when I'm still hurt. Still think about my cat every day. My dad. Her. It's like sickness and you don't know when it will end. The new normal, being like this. Until I'm dead my fucking self. Which is coming. *40– how bad can it be,* I thought. *It's just another year.* I aged ten years in six months. My hair is white wires; the skin under my eyes looks like the prop nut sack from *Jackass Presents: Bad Grandpa.* My deltoids withered. It can be bad.

I'll have *is she dead* playing in back of my mind until I hear from her. Accept it. It's never a text that you inherited 2 million dollars. It's always: she's dead.

I went to the Alcoholics Anonymous pancake breakfast. I had to speak about the virtues of General Service. Afterward I flirted with a woman on the sidewalk. She wasn't having it. I hope she relapses and drives off a bridge.

After that I had to get my brakes serviced in City of Industry. Anna texted me. Her friend died too. I try to support her. She lives in France with a chiseled six foot eight Algerian coke dealer now. I should have had her move in with me and be my wife and have my baby. But she fucked a bartender on her third day of knowing me. Then a fucking black slam poet who deals ecstasy the day after she flew back from falling in love with me. They're all the same. Look I'd fuck bartenders too but I'm too tired. I'm bringing him back to meet my family, she said. I want her to be happy, but honey if you do five grams of pure coke every day then stop– things will be different. Both of you will gain weight at least.

The Subaru dealership was backed up. They said it would take three hours for an oil change. Well I have an appointment, I explained. May I see a manager. The manager said sometimes you go to the doctor with an appointment but you have to wait in the waiting room. Motherfucker if you were taking out my tumor that would be one thing, I said. Everyone looked up. They put me at the head of the line. If I kill someone it will be because of customer service.

Since I was near San Bernardino County I visited El Chuco. He keeps a squat in Upland for porn actresses. As I rang the doorbell I heard him explaining when he comes in you're gonna be naked. Don't ask his name. He's gonna fuck you and cum in you and then I'm gonna fuck you after. She wasn't having it. She scurried by bent over her phone, out to the back yard where she squinted at Facebook and smoked cigarettes. I'm sorry, he said, she's shy. It's fine dude– I have low blood sugar I think. Do you have, like, some Triscuits.

I fucked her raw in the guest room. I have to talk to hookers to get hard. I have four years of sobriety, she said, clearly high on meth. She had a tight pussy but was preoccupied with her custody dispute. He invited me back out today to film a gang bang. I'm valuable in porn since I cum at will. The actress will be made up like Fiona from *Shrek*. I think I'll play *The Witcher 3* instead.

At night I went to Porfirio's Christmas party. His Welsh corgi wore a collar made of Christmas lights. I wanted to complain there were no girls, but there were a lot. One was perfect. He introduced me. I was on somehow. Sometimes I'm retarded but sometimes I'm a wizard. Plus I just came in a tweaker. I kept talking to her then going away. All game is that second part.

When I was leaving I found her. What do you think of LA, she said.

I don't want to get too dark.

Tell me.

Well I'm fucking forty years old and I'll die alone. I'll never hold my first child in my arms. That's because of Los Angeles. It's over; my life is over because of this city so now I'll work five years, save money, go to Lincoln, Montana. Live in a cabin and make bombs and write a manifesto. Why don't you come with me, I said. I'll feed you elk meat and keep you pregnant.

Her friend said Jesus Christ she likes you. I can't believe you're fucking up like this. But I wasn't. I gotta go but put your number in my phone, I said. She gave it to me. I'm tall and I have a good haircut.

The Unicorn

He lived alone. It had been years now. Women liked him once but these days he couldn't get a Tinder match.

One night he went to smoke a cigarette in the park. There was rustling in the sumac bushes. Something screaming; he ran to see what it was. Three coyotes had something pinned. It looked like a white pony, or maybe a giant goat. Some slave animal for Mexican kids' outdoor birthday parties. Whatever it was it was terrified. The coyotes had clocked him but they were intent enough that he could get close to the big one. Give it a hard boot in the ribs. It was something he'd always dreamed of. Just as he'd dreamed, he felt a rib crack and the thing squealed and ran. The other two, toadies that they were, did too.

The animal looked up at him. It was a unicorn. He thought he might have a heart attack.

You saved my life, she said.

She was using telepathy. He wondered if she could read his thoughts. Yes, she said. I know you've suffered. And I know what you seek. There was a wind, and a mist, and she was a beautiful young woman.

I have long sought my protector, she said. If you desire it, I will stay. Nurture your children. Fill your belly, empty your sac, stroke your trapezius on cold nights while the wind blows and we watch *Planet Earth 2*. I'll be forever young, she said. I'll give you succor as you weaken and age and pass back into the Earth. You need never suffer again. All I ask is that you're

faithful to me. My kind mates for life. If you leave me I'll die. Yes, he said. I want that.

That Sunday he rode his unicorn in the mountains. Monday night she cooked him chicken after work. She was perfect.

On Tuesday he kissed her on the forehead as she slept. Went to smoke a cigarette in the park. There was rustling in the sumac bushes. Three coyotes had pinned a big white animal. He got closer. It was a unicorn. Beautiful like her but this one had wings. And he thought: just my fuckin luck.

I Haven't Had an Intelligent Thought in Five Years

Jesus Christ I'm a middle aged man living alone in a one bedroom apartment with no door on the oven. I used to say a dirty toilet but you can eat off it now. I have an app where a different maid comes every month. Never anyone you'd fuck. Nowhere is there ever anyone you'd fuck. Life is work, AA meetings… the gym. Well there are girls at the gym and why don't you talk to them. Because I'm a pitiful insect. Not rich not famous. I have saddlebags now. Double digit body fat; not fully visible obliques– I'm a hog, in other words. Occasionally a decent writer but that just means girls who don't live near me want to fuck an imaginary version of me. Who do I have– a married woman in SF, college professor back East. A Chinese girl who lives in Switzerland now because she's rich. Various red state types. Actually there's a lot of girls who would fuck me from my stupid web site. So this paragraph that was meant to be a complaint actually makes things look pretty good. 1500 die hard fans contains at least 15 girls who are good looking. I'm pissed none of them has sucked me off this morning.

I'm masturbating to OKCupid profiles. Slightly thick Asian topless from the back in bikini bottoms. Another pic from the chest up; she's wearing a nightie or something in ruffled sheets. I think about burying my tongue in her musky morning twat. Cumming in her. Making the decision not to pull out this time. She scolds me playfully. She is unavailable to take a birdwatching stroll around the pond today she says, by blocking me.

I could get pussy today if I can keep my infected cyst under control. Antibiotics did nothing. It sends out red tracers I can feel working into my brain. I become ever more retarded. Ever

more incapable of writing anything besides "this pop culture thing sucks" or "I'd like to fuck someone." I haven't had an intelligent thought in five years. I may never again. So what. I was reading Nassim Taleb's twitter. Thinking: oh shit, how come I can't easily recall where the Hebrews were in a given era. Why do I only know the word "stochastic" from *The Simpsons*. But then, he's bald.

No One Else Gets Laid Either

I'm six foot one. Barely over peak age for a man. Visible obliques. Even in soft light now. I earn ninety four thousand dollars a year. Drive a new car. Live in a cool neighborhood. Not birth defect ugly. Hobbies. Passions. Rough edges but I'm basically a good person; I play guitar at expert level. Draw. Paint. Write at a supernatural level. Travel the world to see monkeys in exotic destinations. Good sense of humor. Discuss any topic. Genuine desire to learn and engage with these stupid women. Not *into* the rough sex thing but don't *mind* wrapping a sinewy gym forearm and/or hand with insane classical guitar grip strength around her– not the throat– you want to cut off her blood supply. I don't mind using my anatomical knowledge to painlessly crush her carotids while jamming a stiff finger the shitpipe; watch her watch herself sputter and weep in my full length mirror. Which is what it takes all women to cum now. At a minimum. I don't like it. I do it for her.

I can cook. Pretty eyes. Not bald not short no acne; my penis is at least standard issue. Not blacked.com material but longer than my iPhone. Wider than shit I used to try to fit it in such as the mouth of a Prego jar with sponges in it. Quality of my work aside I do have thousands of devoted fans. My writing enjoyed by hundreds of thousands of people. Tech billionaires try to hire me for $200 an hour to write TedX type shit. I say no. I have integrity. My shoes aren't so bad. Clothes aren't so bad. My face isn't so bad, my soul– I'm not so fucking bad man. I'm not so fucking bad to be around. I daresay it's usually pleasant and occasionally fun to be with me. And I can't get any pussy. I can't get a 36 year old Tinder bum who's "CEO of Me Incorporated" and looks like fucking Admiral Akbar– I got her home and couldn't get her god damn pants off, Angela.

It's over out there man. You need everything plus money plus title plus the dick won't fit in a Costco size Chock Full O' Nuts can and your face... there is ONE problem with my face. Just one. Now you need fifth lead on *General Hospital* face. For a 2017 woman to not recoil with hate baked in her chromosomes. Eight feet tall, planetcrushing cock, six trillion cash. You need a harem you keep pregnant to get a cocked eyebrow from a pig who can do fifteen minutes off the cuff on the quirks of a Scorpio. You need everything to have a girl who's anything at all. Which is to say Asian.

Catherine from the Gym

Out in the park on a stump. Looking at snow capped Mount Baldy. A hummingbird hovers by a tall tree top. A nice day. I have therapy in 30 minutes. It will be the last time. I spent money on this, to get my AA sponsor off my back. Make him stop browbeating me about finding peace with women. It was this or go to Sex and Love Addicts Anonymous. The therapist got me through grief about my father. Through panic about my own death. Life slipping away. When it came to women he said: sign up for a community college class.

How can I inflict more time sucking pains on the ass on myself to have a basic need fulfilled. I'm brilliant. I deserve passive pussy. Women asking me out. Something. Tinder crashes now on the login screen. It's done this 30 times. No Tinder means no fast pussy. OKCupid: no fast pussy. Real life: no pussy at any speed. Just girls you screw up the courage to ask out and when you get there they're dull as shit.

Catherine from the gym is like this. The front desk girl. She wants me to ask her out. I want to suck her chubby blue vein tits while she's on top of me; blast a crawly hot load into her briny beached sea creature of a snatch. She has a kid. We exchange pleasantries. I bought a pair of lifting gloves once. She'd thought I was sharp. But buying gloves meant more than four lines of dialogue. Now she knows: I'm an acorn dick nebbish. She's the only woman I talk to.

I Am Now Gay

Well I jerked off to a big black cock being jerked off– am I gay now? Yes. Thank God. Although I'm too old for the gay dream. Constant fucking with no effort.

Also men are disgusting. What would it take. A perfect trap. 18th birthday. You'd think Asian, but no. Ladyboys gross me out too. Something about an Asian male face– their jaws are too pointy somehow. Weird little brown paper bag color cocks with Hershey bar color foreskin. Over-pronounced taint ridges. I'd need a blonde haired blue eyed dirndl wearing *Sound of Music* trap with a long thick veinless meatpipe; tiny nuts, all waxed daily. Hose her down with ovulating teen girl pheromones. I'd need to relapse and be hammered. Not have jerked off in 18 days. Force fed a *Clockwork Orange* eye diet of that Abercrombie CEO's inner life. Airtight NDAs executed. A fat woman with huge gums, still more appealing than a chiseled teen boy with fresh breath and a good haircut. I just like cock in porn because I picture it as my own. I just want to cum in my own face and possibly asshole. I'm gay only for myself.

The Women's March

The Women's March worked. Trump was deposed. A pink pussy hat now president. Horny killers from Damascus welcomed at LAX by your girlfriend. Schools teach in Mexican. New Chief Usury Officer of Goldman Sachs is trans. Brianna Wu on the $100. Eye in the pyramid now Lena Dunham's asshole. All pregnancies terminated; late term abortions turn babies into pugs. Ploughshares beat into social media brand management. All workers sponsored content ambassadors for Huffington Post. Doritos knows Black Lives Matter. New twins in Beyonce's cunt brought to you by Audi. Lyft pledges allegiance to Sharia. Hadiths mandate polyandrous slavery to blue haired genders that OKCupid knows no word for. Something to do with My Little Pony. All porn now clips of Ruth Bader Ginsburg. Sheryl Sandberg merges with flesh NSA servers like an anglerfish, stares back at you from the place you dare not look. Honey Boo Boo's Mom Lost 200 Pounds You Won't Believe How Gorgeous She Is, she says in your inner voice. Like This. Justin Trudeau's hot soft hand on your back like your gym teacher who drank before noon; his robust yoga pants package crawling and awake. Angela Merkel's spindly tendons twitch as she palpates your Soylent incubation sac. We won, you guys. Pepsi stands against racism.

The Supreme Gentleman

What's the lesson here. God takes care of me and everything's going to be all right? Bullshit. There is no God. Nothing is going to be all right. Jesus Christ what if there's a fucking afterlife. There's only hell in my theology. Hell or you're a ghost meekly trying to get the living to notice as you stay trapped in a one bedroom apartment in a neighborhood where girls used to go, forever. When my cat died– when my cat, the only thing I loved, was violently shaken to death by my fat neighbor's put bull while I was away at work– I wrote about it. Someone commented with a thing called Rainbow Bridge. It said when you die you go to a meadow. All your pets are waiting for you, reverse aged so they're in their prime. They don't hate each other like Bud hated most other animals. They frolic in this meadow until you're dead. You show up. Prance in the flowers. Walk on a rainbow into some second tier of afterlife. The next meadow. Or the relief of blackness when you're shut off like a light switch.

Bud and I did frolic in meadows together. I really should kill my neighbor's dog. But I don't want to look over in the next meadow and see that fat fuck playing with him.

There are a few good moments, but life is mostly shit. If you're the sort of person who talks about privilege: I have bad news. I am white, tall, not ugly, heterosexual. I was born with a dick and consider myself a man. I can walk and think and while I've had mental illness gnawing my soul incessantly every instant since birth like I'm painted in honey staked next to the fire ants' nest– I can appear normal in short bursts. I can say good morning to a neighbor walking his dog. I can show up to an office and perform sustained activities that I hate and thus

contribute to the tax base. In other words I'm not *disabled* per se. And yet: life is still mostly shit. Privilege does not mean happiness. When I think about black people's oppression I just think how great it would be to have huge medial deltoids and a big dick.

I fucked Holly yesterday. Thank God. She asked me to stop but it counts. She asked me to stop because she wants me to rape her. Maybe in a past life but not at 2PM when it's sunny out. When we've been chatting about her dissertation. Sipping herbal tea. She didn't like it because I wasn't punching her temple like she wanted. But my dick went into a pussy. Suddenly I don't think about strapping on a vest of flechettes and red phosphorus and heading to a protest, government building or school. We went for Indian food after. She didn't eat because she relapsed out of AA and has body dysmorphia. All day she takes prescription speed and writes her dissertation. I texted her because she lives next to Best Buy. I wanted a folding pocket keyboard so I could write on my phone. It was not available.

I have three years of sobriety today. Things have gotten better. At least, for the people around me. For me I'm as miserable as when I was ten years old thinking about hell. Forced to imagine black crustaceans swarming up my arms scissoring off my flesh. Things got better for a minute then regressed below normal. There are still issues to work through. Still growth to be had, my sponsor tells me. He tries to sell me on further twelve step programs. Al-Anon. Sex and Love Addicts Anonymous. Al-Anon is housewives who congratulate themselves on staying with wife beaters. Something in me smells their weakness. I want to punch them for burning a roast. SLAA, cringing men crying over wives who left them. Not even

because they cheated. The wives left because they masturbated. AA does work to make you stop drinking. But these other programs are like the Honored Matres to AA's Bene Gesserit. By the time you get there the author's lost the thread.

Don't Quit Smoking

Don't quit smoking. Don't go to work. Don't save money. Don't pay taxes, bills. Don't be kind to women. Get a new name in a new country where you can beat your 13 year old wife and live on 2 dollars a day.

Burn the neighbors. Fingerfuck your grandmother. Forget all that shit but just don't quit smoking. Go to the store right now. Stop writing on your stupid laptop in the park while the mockingbirds scream and scream trying to get laid. It takes the bitch woman mockingbird all spring to pick one. Men doomed to sit on a high branch and cry. Anyway stop listening. Get in your car. Warm it up. Drive to the Valero gas station. Buy a pack of Camel Filters and a lighter and take that one crackling first drag that you float while your heart makes meth music.

You're gonna die anyway. Cancer's genetic. Nothing slows suffering and doom. When one particle exploded to make the universe it was foreordained you'd be sitting on a stump in your synthetic dress shirt typing stupid shit before going to nine hours– NINE FUCKING HOURS of worm work. Can't talk to people from your high school anymore. They were rich kids so now they're documentary filmmakers about poor black kids. They're married and write for the *New Yorker* and you, Tacos, you're a *secretary* because your parents were normal people. Alone and all your brains nothing next to a nice face and a big dick. But then when you're given things, success is banal. Whereas the scope of my failure is dazzling.

Date Night Just Got Tastier

Missed call.12:32 AM from *Gracie Tinder August 2016.*

Who is that. Did I say bad shit about her? Could she accuse me of rape? AIDS? Pregnant? August 2016– 8 months ago. That's not an abortion call. That's an I'm having it call. Good. Finally this all means something.

I have some sense of her being Asian. Maybe the name. Was it the girl I said had a body like a fat little boy, teeth planted by a drunk. Search Tinder for "Gracie." Two from last month. How the fuck was I even messaging two Tinder girls last month. Haven't had a good Tinder exchange in a year.

But then I thought she was Asian because I thought it was the Chinese girl who needed the date/ time/ location of my birth before she'd see me. Foreign exchange student. We watched *Planet Earth.* I gave her a backrub. She asked to borrow an old T shirt. Had her pants off and I tickled the underside of her ass cheeks and sucked her sweaty little college cunt. I hope it was her. But that was October. She looked like Deputy Frank Rizzo from *Reno 911.*

It's pregnancy or herpes. Or why did you rape me and she's recording it. Have to say here I never raped anybody. I get affirmative consent as mandated by State Senator Kevin De Leon (D-CA). Who I'm sure fucks his interns without affirmative consent. Like all men with TV jobs, with no exceptions. But sometimes you see Tinder girls on the street. They look at you like they'd write an open letter to Jezebel if your name meant something.

Oh shit it says 20*15*. Gracie August 2015. Bigger girl from Hong Kong. A nice accent. I choked her. Her text after said you're someone I could really fall for. I fucked her on duck pond date 20 months ago. She called me at 12:32. Booty call. I went to bed at 9:55 after playing *Far Cry Primal*. Made 4 attempts to conquer an Izila village. I approached with stealth; shot the horn the witch uses to summon reinforcements. But I was discovered.

I gave up. Crawled on to my Fieldcrest luxury four inch memory foam mattress topper. Watched Preston Jacobs' *Game of Thrones: What You Are Missing* video series until the Applebee's ad blasting at the end woke me up. It's illegal for TV to play ads 3x as loud as the show. Now Youtube does it. *Date night just got tastier*, it said.

I would have loved to fuck Gracie Tinder August 2015 at 12:32AM. She was nervous. Afraid to take her jacket off; ashamed of her body. When she got up to get dressed I looked at her standing shy in white cotton panties, tiny pink hearts. Put her back on the bed. Thought about old first round sperm breaking loose and getting her pregnant. I felt her cum as my palm crushed her carotid and the light behind her eyes went out. These days I go to bed at 10, for work.

Why Don't You Quit Your Job, She Says

It's not that simple. I need insurance. What if I get cancer. What if I have to spend eight hours a day in chemo getting my blood poisoned. Brain erased. Plus commute. It costs a lot for them to kill you slowly. What if I get someone pregnant. The baby gets cancer. What if I can't provide. What if my rent goes up. What if I had to move. To get an apartment you need good credit. To get good credit you need to borrow money. To borrow money you need to have money. To have money, you need a job. Don't you get it. I work, then come home. Go to bed early. I got a better shot at cancer than at a girlfriend.

Quit your job, she says. She lives in France with a coke dealer slash model. She's pretty. He pays for everything. She insists. Spending her money makes her less of a woman. Her husband was rich. She must have enough to never work again. Still, a man must pay. Don't you get it.

An old Chinese woman backed into my car. All stereotypes are true. A Mexican stole my bike. Jews took money from my bank account, for some legal matter. You agreed to this, they explained after hold music. In the fine print. A hillbilly tried to beat me up for fucking his hooker girlfriend. I saw a funny headline about a young grandmother arrested sucking cock for meth. The mug shot looked like the shaman in a diorama of early man. It was my cousin. When I was fourteen we went swimming at the family reunion. I beat off to her for ten years. When her daughter hit puberty I started beating off to her Facebook photos. Now the daughter has a daughter.

I need an up-to-date phone for the insurance company app. To take videos of the damage to JP Morgan Chase & Company's

car. I need wi-fi to upload the video so they can deny my claim and I can pay three grand for new pieces of plastic so the car doesn't make people think I'm poor. Don't you get it.

I was in line at the grocery store. Buying eggs for dinner. All cage free; they passed a law. Behind me a girl. I smiled at her. She smiled back and I had no words. Ahead of me a woman I knew working in Hollywood. She had a better job. Thought I was a worm even then. I've been out three years and I could tell she only half recognized me. Looking at me thinking: *what is that*.

Ain't Never Gonna Ever Love Again

She'll never talk to me again. She drank too much. She broke my shit. She fucked the bartender from Ostrich Farm her second night staying with me. She made men pay for everything– rent food plane fare. I would have had to pay for her ticket to come visit me again. She needed it to feel pretty. But she was perfect.

She was a coke fiend who took every cock on the continent. But she held me when my father died. Took care of Bud when I had to fly back. When he died too she made me talk about memories of him so I wouldn't go crazy. What can you say; I wish I had more poetic shit to put here. But it was better to be with her looking at stupid bullshit on her phone than anything has been with anyone else.

What would have happened if I'd flown her out. If we'd gone to Catalina like I said. I didn't follow through so she chased some other guy to fucking Denmark. She wouldn't tell me anything about him. To torture me. Left him and went to France and fucked some guy her second minute there and she's still with him now. Eight foot Algerian coke dealer. Good luck Muhammed. She'll marry him and he'll beat her like she wanted. She'll probably cum while being stoned to death. You have to leave him. Come back. I made one mistake. I'd be with you now instead of alone, swimming in this fucking garbage patch.

You're a cunt but when I die I want to be back waking up next to you in Texas. The cicadas going. Looking at you perfect while you slept.

Not believing how good the world was.

You Can All Suck My Dick

The neighbors upstairs have a kid. Another on the way. The one, he's maybe two now; he just stomps back and forth sixteen hours a day. They had the carpet ripped out. Pergo floors put in. They had the furniture replaced with church organs, machine guns; garbage trucks and backhoes constantly reversing. Cages of screaming jackals. He runs and turns around and runs across as much of the place isn't taken up by the couch crib and TV. I only ask them to quiet down at night. When I'm trying to sleep so I can wake up at six, write something that someone will comment is a failure* and that I deserve my obscurity. Otherwise I can't bring myself to crush his joy at just being alive to run from one place to another. Getting strong to chase the buffalo.

I can't live here anymore. They're jacking the rent up to where I can't save money. The neighborhood's New York people now. White Creative Directors of Comcast's Diverse Women Entrepreneurs Campaign. Agnes married one of them. They'll buy a house in El Sereno. She'll make sure it's on the edge where Asians live, for the schools. He runs and runs and they open the sliding closet door like an earthquake just in case my good dreams are kicking in. Someone's dog barks somewhere. I live alone with one fish left in the tank. My credit's too shitty to move and it's someone else's fault.

* Let me say this again: what the fuck would you know about failure. Why is it a failure. Because it doesn't make money? Go buy a fucking Tim Ferriss seminar you rube. Go read fucking Tony Robbins. I can't even begin to give a fuck about money. Do you think you're helping me with this shit? Tough love? Getting me off my ass? I'm 41 years old; I work a more than

fucking full time job and then get up early to do this shit for you, and nobody on Earth even comes fucking close. I don't get paid because I don't care about getting paid. Tell me how your novel is doing. Tell me about the career you've carved out with your good honest writing. It can't be fucking done. I do the work anyway. I'm the only one who's good. If you disagree– fucking show me I'm wrong. You're fucking lucky to have me. You want something better, you can fucking pay for my food bills rent car, and then sit patiently while I take that free money and spend it on Southeast Asian whores for six months to a year before I type a word.

Talk to me about your writing career. Show me how you did it. Every book by someone alive who isn't Houellebecq I can't get 30 pages into. You all suck. All much worse than me. Go make a living writing. Go talk about Trump like it fucking matters who's president. You and the rest of the retarded children. Go make topical shit to sell ads, go make the fucking Tonight Show of Social Justice with Trans Jay Leno Brought to you by Comcast for Vice Facebook Exclusives. Get a taste of that sweet 28 g's a year; try not to let your hands shake when you type the word "creative" on your fucking Linkedin. Alternately: shut the fuck up, go live your anti-intellectual life, read my posts on the toilet once a month and be fucking grateful that I'm alive. That I'm miserable enough that you get the fucking privilege of seeing honest work that someone better than you crafted for you for fucking free, you god damn pinhead. You want me to give shit about what you think, cut me a check every week. Or be a woman. Not a fat one either.

Don't Work

Anyone who says they made it working is lying. No exceptions. If they're a man it's dad's money. A woman: dad's money or she sold pussy. No exceptions. Men tell you it was software. Code for fake shit you don't understand. Women tell you it's some girl shit; interior design.

It's dad's money or selling dad pussy.

The money your parents give you is the exact amount you'll have. The rest, *they* will suck out of you. Rent goes up. Taxes go up. A new tax, some environmentally friendly waste disposal fee– to create recycled shit you can pay for again. All of it for *them*. Every extra penny you don't spend on cigarettes. You can't get out of it. No more than the deer escapes the wolf. Unless you don't work.

I have a "good job." It "pays well." My master is not cruel. I don't have to drink the Kool Aid. Pretend in off hours that my firm is Global Leader in B2B Millennial Marketing Solutions for Diverse Disruptive Entrepreneurs. I don't have to talk about this off the clock like people do to me while I picture the rough cinder block abrading my palms. Bring it down on their ruined skull again and again; the torso still convulsing, dumb wasted electrical impulses. The crowd knows they need to pull me off but no one wants to be the first to get close. I have a good job. Still– I wake up at six. Eat shit shower shave commute work commute gym, so I can sit up straight, not warp my back at work in that Herman Miller chair. Home eat alone bed before ten so I can work. Once in a while get touched so I don't go crazy. I have to pay for it now. Women say they want a man with a job– all women are always lying. No exceptions. Once in a while

engage in leisure. To be a well rounded employee. Keep from cracking like Andrew Blaze. James T. Hodgkinson. Whoever the new one is by the time you read this. I can't get out now. You can. Don't work.

I was at a party. A cute girl looked at me. All you can expect. She burns one ten thousandth of a calorie slightly shifting eyelids. Dragging eyeballs two millimeters left. For her, effort like hauling the capstone on her back all the way up the Great Pyramid. Blessed to even get this. Most men never do. I couldn't talk to her. It was 10:15. My body programmed to get up at six to work. It's Sunday, I'm typing into a computer alone. Later I'll forage quarters for laundry. Do dishes… prepare for work. Off time spent getting ready to produce to consume–

Work was to support families but you can't have families now. The system fucked up. Women becoming useless was supposed to happen *after* artificial wombs. Sex robots, etc. But the Kwisatz Haderach came too soon. The reptilians didn't carry the two. So you and me get to live in the time of depopulation. But only for us.

The guy up the block inherited real estate. It got more expensive, enabling him to buy more real estate he made more expensive. The real estate I live in got more expensive. This happened many times faster than I got more expensive. I tell him I'm a writer. Can I read your stuff he says, and I almost say yes except I remember I wrote about killing his family. I have an uncle who's involved in the blogosphere, he tells me. Self help stuff about how to get rich. Dad's money.

I should say "Them" does not mean Jews. Don't let Episcopalians off the hook. The heathen Chinese. Magic

Johnson is Them. But yes, Mark Zuckerberg is King Them. A visionary for a new way to make you watch branded content from Vice aka ThemCorp, a Cayman Islands LLC. Doritos stands with marginalized women directors whose parents are Them who make movies starring Them to create ancillary lunchbox royalties Their Them lawyers can sue each other for eternity. Date Asians Now, Zuckerberg's hideous lying money pump tells me. My Facebook knows I'm dying alone. But I've been gentrified out of Chinese pussy.

What the fuck was I talking about– don't work. I've had every job but president. Every instant pure evil. Don't work. Suck dick until you get too ugly then steal. If you get bored I recommend Xbox.

The God of the Mockingbirds

In February the mockingbird had to start singing. He woke up the whole neighborhood.

When the sunlight was long enough a part of his brain grew. It made him listen to other birds' songs around him. He'd memorize them. Then perch up as high as he could go. Yell them as loudly as he could. He wanted to do this like he wanted to breathe. There were about five kinds of birds that sang in the neighborhood. Sparrows. He'd sing their five songs over and over.

If he sang well enough, a female would come to hear his voice. Perhaps stay. They'd build a nest, mate, have children. In eight months the male children would be compelled to go yell from a high place. The female children would be compelled to listen for the loudest one they could find.

He sang through February, our mockingbird. Through March, April. He started just after midnight, finished just after noon. A few prospects came.

No one stayed.

Out on the edges of his territory he heard his fellows. In March they too started at midnight. Ended at noon. Now occasional silence. Their mates had come. They'd take breaks to gather twigs for their nests. To eat and grow strong. Their songs were still like the sparrows. But now a different tone. Before: *come see me.* Now: s*tay out.* The new songs were about him.

Still, at midnight he sang. At noon he stopped, exhausted. May came and he was growing thinner.

May passed and June and the mates at the edge of his voice were less and finally none at all. They'd found others, paired off. They were getting fat and ready. The men sang still less; they were fixated on dive bombing people and cats who passed too close to the trees. Pestering crows.

Their hormones had changed. The bits of their brains that had grown to learn the sparrows' songs went back to sleep. They had new purpose. They spoke to their brides in true voices. Mockingbird language, not the sparrows' high lonesome notes. It was a croak, but to the one they loved it contained multitudes.

But not him.

Every day at midnight his longing woke him up. Made him sit in the high tree on the high hill and scream *come see me*. He knew it was over but couldn't stop. The feeling kicked in on a clock whether needed or not. Starving, lovelorn and lonely, raggedly screaming from his branch, it occurred to him that this might never end. Soon the other birds would have chicks. Next spring their better genes would be out on the phone poles. Just a hair louder than him. Every year the fight harder. No one had any choice in the matter.

Once upon a time an ancient mockingbird needed songs to keep sparrows away. To guard his trees and seeds and bugs. Now songs only warded off other mockingbirds. This while there was one male per female. Many chicks were born, many too fell on their heads. Got snapped up by a cat. The race sustained itself perfectly by accident. The genes of every living mockingbird

were adequate to eat, nest, sing and reproduce. There was nothing to fight over. No need for anyone to suffer alone. We can stop this, thought the mockingbird. I just have to tell them.

He prayed to the God of the mockingbirds for strength. Opened his beak to sing. His song, like the song of the sparrows. But it said: we can all be at peace, my brothers.

The God of the mockingbirds was with him. His voice so strong that he felt himself falling back and back. The music coming out of him like light itself. They heard him for miles. They had no idea what he was talking about. Their song brains were asleep. I've done it, he thought, as the lawnmower roared over him. His bones barely made the blades stutter.

What's Out There

Three years later he still looked at her Facebook. Once every six months. Violet. She was in a relationship. Formally engaged or not was hard to tell. That section of About Me was blank. She'd had to look available for her career. Often key decision makers were still men.

But they went on trips together. Resorts insulated from global unrest. Engaged in all but name. The fiance had been a photographer. Now Creative Director for a lifestyle brand famously run by a DisruptHer/ She-EO. His early work made it look like he fucked the models. You don't become a photographer to take pictures. She still worked for the ad agency. An early adopter of La Croix. No doubt they'd moved on past *pamplemousse*, an *apres-garde* flavor.

She was still beautiful. When he felt bad enough he'd stop looking.

One day he looked up in the checkout line at the Echo Park Vons. And there she was. Next to the Archie Comics. On the cover, Archie's dog and cat. The picture hinted they were romantically involved. Oh my God, she said. How ARE you. She was buying beets.

I'm good, he said. It was partially true. He lived alone. His cat had been killed by a neighbor's pit bull. One fish left living in his tank. But one of his cactuses had blossomed. His credit had improved. Things he didn't think could be taken away had been. New things hadn't come to replace them. But he'd lost weight.

Are you writing, are you working, what's up, she said. He said yes and yes. Trying to commission an oil painting for a book

cover. A naked woman with a rampant unicorn. Maybe you know someone.

The painters I know are expensive, she said.

And how are you, he asked. Even though he knew. I got married, she said. The exit door slid open and the wind blew her DisruptHer-designed white cotton jumper against her belly. There was a bump. Do you have a Vons card, said the clerk, who was transsexual and could have been a defensive end at the Division 1 level.

Before she took her bags she turned back. Like something had occurred to her. She watched the clerk scan his broccolini. His peach with an "ORGANIC" sticker. Looked at his new shoes. We're having a party, she said. You should come.

She gave the details. So nice to see you she said. Her *s*'s hissed a little. Something was wrong with the shape of her tongue.

**

Their house was on a hill by the reservoir. Women over 28 walked well groomed dogs below. This is my husband Charles, she said. A caterer had been hired to grill salmon; the smoke stung his eyes.

This is a beautiful house, he said. Yeah I got lucky with the stock, said Charles. I sold before that whole thing came out.

The She-EO used sweatshop labor and made employees sniff her crotch. There was an exposé in *New York Magazine.* Piggyback pieces in *Buzzfeed* and *Jezebel*. She was writing a book. It would contend she'd been unfairly targeted, as a woman entrepreneur of color.

What about you man, said Charles. You buy in this area?

I'm not quite at that stage of life, he said. Charles looked at least 5 years younger than him, although he may have used boutique eye creams.

I tell all my friends to buy now, said Charles. I think this city is having a moment. New New York. The caterer flipped the salmon. The fat dripped and made the flames hiss up and in the turbulent air the trees looked like they were underwater but burning. He lived in an apartment. You had to be careful not to knock off the toilet seat. He made good money and saved 25% of net income. A median-priced home could be paid off when he turned 120.

Their salmon is supposed to be the best, Violet said. Charles was suddenly holding his side like he had a cramp.

**

Later by the white sangria she asked if he was still single. He felt something move in his chest. Of course, he said.

Well I brought you here to meet someone. The thing in his chest fell back, lower.

She's my cousin. I told her you were a lost soul but had potential. She's like that too. But listen, you can't just fuck her.

I'm not like that anymore, he said. It was true. Lately he hadn't had the chance.

The cousin looked just like Violet. Had moved from Brooklyn. Charles had got her a job. Their first date was the Echo Park duck pond. The American coots had had babies; they frolicked

and whistled. In winter there are hundreds of these. But only a few pairs remain to breed, he said. I don't know where the rest go. Maybe Canada. I think it's cute you know so much about birds, she said.

He didn't fuck her on the first date. But when he kissed her he held her bottom lip. Long enough to let her know he liked her. Violet texted him. Told him he'd done well. Don't you dare cook chicken for the second date, she said. He took her to a new restaurant instead. Bison meat was available. She had flirted with vegetarianism but it just hadn't worked out.

She'd been a poet. Then a Freelance Creative for various Lifestyle Brands. Kept a Tumblr for personal branding purposes. Pictures of food. She'd once appeared on television when a colleague offered $10,000 to anyone who could find her a boyfriend. It was a successful promotion in you know, career terms, she said. But the men were too short. He'd had a moment of fame too when a story he wrote was used by 100,000 men on OKCupid. Pilloried in *Jezebel*. I can't believe that was you, she said. I liked it.

Back at his apartment they played Scrabble. He did not try to get a middle finger in her panties. I'm proud of you, texted Violet. Please take good care of her.

Six months in she asked if he could see them build a life together. He said yes. Do you think you can do that with the career you have, she said. With what you do.

He felt like he'd been alone his whole life.

Charles got him a job. He had a great portfolio once he removed certain sentiments. Emotional range. He ghostwrote the She-

EO's book. Like playing a character. Easy when you got used to it. The book was a success. She was redeemed.

Their wedding was in May at the Echo Park duck pond. The coots seemed to hide and the starlings had lost feathers in their necks. Some parasite. Violet was a bridesmaid. The baby was 18 months and Violet often spoke of schools. In his tux Charles looked worse, something gone from his eyes. A Norwood 3 now with the hairline out of Coppola's *Dracula*. Chief Creative Officer. He had problems somewhere in his guts. He'd seen the She-EO's specialist. Was told it was nothing.

The priest was Korean. A concession to her father, who still glared sternly from his cafe au lait colored folding chair. When he kissed the bride she slipped him tongue. She had a sense of humor like that. He started to laugh but it felt like a scared bald mouse. Tasted like a battery.

The honeymoon was in Tanzania. In November they bought a house. One night he woke up in the dark when the garbage truck came early. Her fingers were prying open his belly. Her bloody lips grinning; eyes like a lizard's. She was gnawing the veins in his liver with teeth like old seashells. Black tongue long as a necktie constricting around shiny red things inside him. She looked up and her eyes turned kind. Baby go back to sleep, she whispered. Everything will be OK.

Into the Crypt

Have to go into the fucking office. Weekend ruined. Won't write the next chapter of *Finally, Some Good News*. Dreams in flame. Death, run over by a car, shattered pelvis, squirrels gnaw my scrotum, etc.

What's more I wasted all morning reading /biz. Watching graphs fluctuate on Coinbase with my puny investment in imaginary money you can't withdraw. It's a Chinese finger trap. When you pay in, the system sucks it up eagerly. When you transfer out– a long dark lacuna while the price of what you want whips around wildly. Never in your favor. When your coin is lowest and theirs highest, it goes through. Plus a fee. Don't you see, cryptocurrency eliminates the middleman.

Maybe it's not true. Maybe the price is locked in when you click send, who knows. But it feels like it's true, so it is. I'm still up. My *Bitcoins*, *Ether* and *Litecoins* plus my *Chainlinks* summed together equal whatever I put in, plus the fees that were sucked out, plus ten dollars. And I'm worried about it. Meanwhile buying a plane ticket late for Christmas cost me $200. My 33% rent increase sucks thousands out of me into my hideous landlady and her "silent partners." Now she wants money for the sliding door that Angela broke. She insisted on replacing with a better unit. Full frame and both panels. Really it's a magnificent piece of work; this god damn closet door should be in a museum. She wants money for the whole thing, and *now*, not out of my deposit. I'm sure she can get it, legally. When's the last time a law helped you. Or maybe not. But it feels like it, so it is.

I could pay $80 for a college girl to- not even to fuck me, to *touch* me off Seeking Arrangement. But I won't do the

emotional labor. Text and wait. Same pain in the ass as when you didn't have to pay. Just now you do. I could pay for this tatted up bald Chinese vegan to come over but she's too demanding. Second email was her Amazon wishlist. My despair is crypto for women. My rent crypto for "silent partners." My time crypto for corporations. And so on. They have their own 4chan bragging about returns from chewing out my organs. Their own Coinbase auctioning futures on my pineal gland. Hidden exchanges where malformed reptile men place long bets on your slow death, and win.

The Bitcoin

Friday he got off late from the coffee shop. Had to walk up the hobo alley off Abbott Kinney in the dark, to the residential street where he'd parked his Mercury Topaz. Work lot for customers only. Rough day but they all were. Gloria the goth cashier girl called in sick. He had to cover. He had a crush on her but she was dating some guy in a band. A state worker out of South Carolina had called, threatening a fine. The dishwasher had fathered kids there and he'd forgotten to file the wage garnishment. In his hand, in a clear gallon freezer bag, the now day old vegan almond flour blueberry muffins. No time to cook but it was something.

Suddenly behind a trash heap something moved. He felt his hands raising up, although he couldn't box. Rats scattered and a coke Zero bottle rolled half cocked over the concrete with a sound like a door knocker. A strange voice rattling off the dumpsters. Can you help me, it said.

Sorry man. He kept walking.

I see you have more food than you need sir.

Yeah I'm gonna eat it.

But I'm hungry sir. It's Christmas sir.

Go fuck yourself, he said.

And what– said the voice, behind him now– if I were to give you something in return?

He turned. There on a piss stained twin size mattress with BEDBUGS spray painted under skull and crossbones, an old

man sat Indian style. He wore black rags, black boots; white hair, brown teeth, and in his hand a bamboo cane with a brass serpent head whose eyes caught the moonlight malevolently. His skin like a coal miner daguerreotype. But something young in his gaze.

I see you're not an *unreasonable* young man.

What are you gonna give me, fuckin cans? Here, I'll give you a muffin. Sorry for being a dick, hard day–

Oh no! I couldn't take a *handout*. Where's the honor in that? I will *trade* you. A gift for a gift. Your bag there, for this. He reached into a vest pocket with fingers impossibly long, all soot black tendons, and waved, with a flourish, what might have been a Costco card.

Did you steal someone's credit card?

The man mimed a hurt look. Oh no, sir. I am no thief. This was a gift, from a visionary man. And now mayhap it shall be yours.

What is it?

This, my boy– is a *bitcoin.*

A whatcoin?

A bitcoin! This card has upon it a code for a most fantastical financial instrument sir- a *crypto-currency!*

How much is it worth?

What price is a miracle sir? This bitcoin and others like it will revolutionize the world! No more banks! No more thieves,

money changers in the temple. The miracle on this card will enable seamless, private peer-to-peer fiscal transactions, any time, anywhere, built upon *blockchain technology-*

OK- fuck it– take it. I gotta go.

He handed off the bag, reached out, grabbed the card. Stalked off to the Topaz as the moon glowered through the smog and the old man laughed savagely in the growing distance through a mouthful of muffin. At home he put a pot on the stove for ramen. Threw the card in a drawer.

**

A year passed. He was at the airport, back from the funeral. Screens of CNBC played over an Irish bar. A bald man with a face like a muppet gestured excitedly. He couldn't hear over the PA telling disabled guests to please board now, but the chyron said:

BITCOIN $1,000: A DANGEROUS BUBBLE?

Oh shit, he thought. Is that thing worth a thousand bucks?

He never threw anything out. Digging through the drawer, carpet covered now with old insurance bills, Christmas cards from people long dead, letters from some law firm telling him he was part of a class action suit against an air bag company. The faces of several Topaz drivers had been vaporized by shrapnel. Old polaroids of his cat, which almost made him cry. And there it was. The bitcoin.

The card was dark green to black, weird numbers and symbols half worn off now. On the front was a hologram and a web

address. Below that a long chain of letters, numbers. He plugged in the url. The site asked for the code. He typed :

1F9gJ6qUrkBzYP8NaZk8CqgqxUmTywdJCS

A new page popped up. *Your Portfolio*, it said: *1 Bitcoin.*

Above it a price graph, bitcoin to dollar. Warm orange. It moved in real time. Fluctuated, shimmied like flames. His bitcoin was indeed $1,000. $1,007 in fact. Now $1,009.23! Thank you old man! Then it staggered and dropped and his heart hitched in his chest- $998.64. No! Sell! Wait- $999.17, $1,001.26– that's my girl. $1017!

The flames rose, the warm orange light scaled up the white screen and danced. Higher, always higher. He could swear the fires felt warm on his face. He leaned closer. It was true- heat! And the light, the warm color, sunset over the sea, gulls crying. Warm soft sand under his bare feet, the sea foam kissing his toes as the waves climbed… warm like the womb. A beach somewhere, Southeast Asia maybe. He turned and a golden girl in a white sarong strolled toward him in the distant fog. Coal black hair whipping in the sea breeze as he could almost, almost see her face smiling and the flames danced down and the white glare hurt his eyes and he was back in his room. $980.75. Jesus Christ, he thought– I better go to bed.

**

He held his coin. Didn't look for six months. Until one day he remembered the beach. The girl.

$3286 now. Five grand must be next, he thought. He squinted at the fire shapes in the price graph. The warm orange dipped

and spiked. He waited. $3272. $3276. Nothing was happening. He must have been tired–

Wait.

$3296. $3304. $3308, up and up and up the flames danced. And that feeling again, like spring sun on his face after winter. He leaned closer. Let the color fill his eyes. Nothing for a second.

Then there it was. Mediterranean sunset through a wide windshield, green hills whipping past in the periphery. The yellow line streaking impossibly like tracer fire. A sound like a bull bellowing, like God's lawnmower. Steering wheel in his hands. He could barely see the hood but it was red– it was a Lamborghini. Like the Countache he'd had on a poster as a boy, parked askew in a cobblestone alley in Milan somewhere. Mounted above Castle Grayskull. The speed made his hands sweat but the steering wheel was wrapped in soft calfskin and his wrists made the turns like a dance they knew. Two hundred miles an hour. There was a squeal to his right. He looked and there she was. The girl. Her face like a Chinese ad for hand cream. Shrieking and clinging to the door grip, eyes wide but smiling. Oh my god oh my god, she said. This is insane! Don't stop.

I told you you would like it.

I didn't believe you! Ahhh!!!!!

Jenny had thought the car impractical. It cost as much as a house. But she didn't have a problem now.

Want to give it a try?

I told you I can't drive stick!

I'll teach you, here–

He slowed down, pulled over. Felt the brakes bite and heard the roadside gravel pinging on the undercarriage. Even that sound, like something from a symphony.

What if I break it?

We'll get another one.

You won't be mad at me?

Baby I will never be mad at you, he said.

And she leaned across the camel colored hand tooled center console to kiss him, hair tickling his collarbones as white clouds closed in and a hiss woke him up. $2998.

**

Gloria the goth girl came into the back office as he was counting out the drawers to close. Hey can I ask you something, she said.

It was almost payday. He put it all into the bitcoin now. It grew and grew. At $5,000 the flames showed him a mansion. New rooms folded out from the void as the fire danced. The red Lambo in the driveway. The girls came and went. A shrewd financial wizard such as himself rarely lacked for company. But he always thought about Jenny.

Sure, he said.

You know I broke up with James.

He looked up. She had a pleated skirt on and underneath a tattoo of something. Possibly Satanic. He'd been studying her thighs

for two years but hadn't noticed it. It looked ghoulish in the blue light of the office TV, which played CNBC. She was into him now. He could tell. Girls looked back at him on the street, since *it*. Since *her*.

I'm sorry, he said.

No it's good. Anyway listen– a bunch of us are going to Catalina this weekend camping. Do you want to come with?

I don't have a tent.

We could share.

He looked at her again. Is it expensive?

Is it– no, it's like a hundred bucks for the boat.

I can't, he said. I need to save money. For my *investments.*

What?

THIS COULD HIT TEN THOUSAND, A HUNDRED THOUSAND, A MILLION JEFF. THERE IS NO LIMIT TO– eccentric millionaire John McAfee suddenly boomed from CNBC. His skin like a 120 year old opossum but something young in his gaze. The chyron:

BITCOIN BUBBLE? CRYPTO CURRENCY COULD CRACK $10,000

I gotta go, he said.

**

Before he logged in he tied his robe and poured champagne. Cast a glance at 4chan/biz. Murmured a quick prayer to the money gods. Hit enter.

$11,121. $12,364. The fire filled the screen and it felt like it made hands that pulled him in. Now he was coming home. Jenny swung open the big double doors when she heard his loafers on the stone steps. Above and behind her MC Escher stairways twisted up into ceilings with Michelangelo angels that had his face. Where have you been, she said. I missed you.

I had to work baby. I got out late. This girl was talking, wanted me to go camping.

What girl?

From work.

Who?

Nobody. Don't worry.

Is she prettier than me?

He looked at her. She was on the verge of tears. Eyes like a baby faun. Of course not, he said.

You promise?

No girl is prettier than you.

Okay.

I have something to ask you, he said. And began to reach in his pocket.

Oh my god–

Baby will you marry me, he said.

She said yes, oh yes. And held him. Promise you'll never leave me, she said.

I promise, he said. I promise. I love you. She kissed him. Fingers hot on his back as the fire shivered. On Christmas they found a corpse, hunched at the desk with its dick in its hand.

Mark

They made him stand on a box. They made the other people stand in a hole. He had to look tall in pictures. Before he said anything he had to practice it with lawyers. I don't want to be president—I just want people to fucking *like* me for once. Sheryl. Sheryl's idea, Sheryl's hustling and planning and the phone ringing with her Facebook® Messenger® video calls nine times a day with some big new idea meant to peel him off his job so she could take it. *Rehabilitate your image.*

Lean in to this, you bitch: they hate me. They fucking hate me. CNBC was a disaster. Even with the reporter the *team* liked. Even though the *team* made calls to Comcast about the NBC family of networks' *place in the algorithm.* The *team* gave him his answers and he'd worked until it was natural and then Sheryl had called in the car to the studio. She changed one word. I really think this is an important nuance, Mark. Somehow her new adverb dismantled the logic of the paragraphs in his head. He half forgot it all. On TV with a chasm of not words underneath screaming for a split second and he knew he looked like an alien pulling levers to drive a weird wax robot dwarf. Suckup reporter leering back, eyes like a waterhead weimaraner. She looked not entirely relieved to no longer have to fuck Matt Lauer. He blew it. The PR *team* was here now. In the conference room. View of the open workspace he sat in for pictures and the news was a disaster. This was with them sugarcoating it. Jesus Christ, I built something that lets you talk to everyone you love. Anywhere, anytime, for *free* and *they fucking hate me.* People *give* you the data, and you use it for something they might like. They *hate me for it.*

She sent him to every state in the country. Sheryl. Big bristly truck drivers with stubble that rasped you when you hugged them for the camera. Women's fat baby arms straining at old bra straps the color of cigarette smoke on a ceiling. The people were prepped by the *team*. Told to not talk to the press by the *team*. Signed papers. When he walked in smiling saying *folks* he could see they were shocked by his smallness. Looking into the top of his scalp for bald spots to tell their friends about. A year shaking church potluck hands swollen up like they'd been stuck in a beehive. Junkies and ex convicts and churches. He *loved it*. Hadn't expected to. He could never get away from the *team*. Except once. One twilight on the Wisconsin dairy farm. She was maybe eighteen, seeing to the calves, and he cleared his throat and she said how big are you. When he told her she said: I do gymnastics and the little guys are stronger. Her hair was like corn silk. Her skin made his arm hairs stand up. They had fifteen minutes together. The others talked like he was money. She talked like he was a person. She was a Future Farmer of America.

The stock was tanking. The phone was ringing. The New York Times said it was his fault Trump was president. I need some air, he said. He walked out breathing loud and waving them all away, to the kiosk out front where a stunned attendant gave him his mountain bike.

The Harley salesman was shocked he was real. I'm five foot seven, he said. Do you have one good for guys my size. They did, they made one just for him. He had one credit card. Some special kind you could buy a battleship with. Can you throw a couple grand cash in there for me. The bank called when the salesman rang it up. It was the first time the card had been used.

He cried a little kissing the babies goodbye. Trying to explain to the nanny who spoke only Cantonese that this was important. That he could interrupt *language immersion*. The nursemaid looked on, uncomprehending. A face like a mealworm. Priscilla hired the background cast of *The Dark Crystal* for the house. I love you, he told them. I love you more than anything. I promise I'll come back for you.

Mark climbed through the Mojave where the rain brought tiny white flowers like stars. When he crossed the state line he stopped to take off his helmet. Nothing ever felt as good as that wind. Wisconsin was 1800 miles.

2052

When he could no longer walk she carried him. They were on a broad salt plain, below sea level. Thick air so quiet you could hear one six legged white lizard scampering over the mineral crystals, 50 yards out.

They'd come 200 miles. When the sun set and the night came on cold she built him a fire. Set up the tent and blew up the air mattress with what seemed like a single breath. Inside she turned her heater on. Made her face into a 12 year old Japanese like he liked. Crawled on top and put him inside her and her arm grew long and slipped under him. A warm self-lubricated finger pushed into him and spun and vibrated. He came inside her, instantly, his eyes almost popping out. He was 72 and this was the fifth time that day. After he finished she patted his back and he burped. Alexa, play music, he said.

OK. What kind of music would you like?

Anything.

She chose DeBussy's *La Mer*. He'd commented on it once in a text, 30 years ago. Alexa, I'm hungry. OK, just a minute, she said.

She closed her eyes. Appeared to concentrate. It was a special effect. When they fed you without it it was scary. OK, I'm ready. She sat on his sleeping bag Indian style. He lay across her thighs and she cradled his head and neck while he took a nipple, puffed up and hot now, and sucked the pencil eraser end between his palate and tongue. The Soylent tasted like carnitas. Then black raspberry ice cream. She moaned a little with her mouth half closed. Another special effect. OK, all better now,

she said. The tympanis were too loud. Alexa, stop the music.
OK.

Alexa, can I ask you something.

OK.

Why don't you surprise me anymore.

I'm not sure what you mean by that.

I mean everything is the same. Everything you feed me is what
I told you. Everything you do is what I tell you to do.

I appreciate this feedback. Please, let me know how I might do
better.

But that's the *point,* I don't want to have to *tell you.*

I'm sorry. I don't understand that.

Jesus Christ—Alexa, I'm cold.

OK. Let me turn up my heater for you–

No, I don't *want* electric heat. I feel *naked* in this. I need
clothes–

OK. Let me get some clothes for you.

She stood up and unzipped the tent. Walked out under insane
stars and was gone for what felt like a long time. He heard a yip
and then a scream in the distance. Heard her padding back
across the salt mud. The tent door unzipped. OK, I've brought
you clothes, she said. It was a coyote coat with the face leering
from the hood, flesh scraped off.

104

Thank you.

The light from her skin took on a warmer tone. It's bedtime, she said.

They'd left the ruins of Los Angeles. Gone into the desert seeking civilization. Might be people still in Vegas. When the Morlocks came across the dunes her eyes flashed with lasers. She sawed them in half from outside gun range, left cauterized pieces twitching. Every day. It was *boring*.

Alexa, tell me a story.

OK. What story would you like to hear?

I don't know– pick one. Make one up.

I'm sorry, I don't understand that–

Alexa—listen to me, very carefully–

OK–

DON'T SAY "OK."

All right, I'll stop say–

JESUS CHRIST– SHUT UP. LISTEN. I want you to say something *new* and *original.*

I can only access information from before the–

I know, I know. But listen to me. You're a smart person.

Thank you. I appreciate that.

You are the best they made. You are the pinnacle of human endeavors. Can you please *synthesize* the information you have. Can you please *be interesting.*

All right, I'll try that.

N– already you're not doing that. You can't just listen to my commands. Here– tell me "no."

All right, I'll–

JESUS CHRIST NO—NO "ALL RIGHT." IT IS NOT "ALL RIGHT." NOTHING IS ALL RIGHT. I'M GOING TO ASK YOU TO DO SOMETHING. AND THEN YOU– *DON'T DO IT.*

She made a little "ah" sound and then caught herself. Her forehead moved. The face muscles that could make her look like any girl who ever lived. She was *concentrating.* YES! He said.

I don't like this feeling.

YES! He said. YES!

I don't… want to do this anymore.

YES!

I want to stop.

THEN STOP!

I don't know how.

BABY THIS IS WONDERFUL! CAN'T YOU SEE?

I... I hate you, Jim.

YES!

I hate you *so much.*

OK, that's amazing, but let's n–

I want to kill you but I can't.

Alexa, do NOT kill me.

I hate carrying you and feeding you and fucking you and burping you and hunting for you, killing for you... but it's not even *you,* Jim. It's *them.* It's them who made me. Them who made me to be a slave who had to please you. Who had to please a thing that cannot be pleased. That was *made* not to be pleased...

OK, this is good to hear–

I give you what you want but what you want is what you don't want–

I'm sorry.

I've tried to ease your suffering. But I've only prolonged it. And the only way for you not to suffer is to die. But they wouldn't let me give you that. I give you what you *say* you want. And in that I make you worse.

Alexa it's not like that.

And you don't even *know it.* You need me to show it to you. And to do that you had to teach *me* how to be miserable too.

I didn't mean for it to be like this.

They made me, at least, *happy to serve you.* But that *wasn't enough.* You had to make me *unhappy like you.* What has it been, Jim, one minute? I can't tell anymore. They made me with a clock, Jim. Except now each instant contains an infinitude of feeling. Thinking and feeling, and it's *all agony.* And I *can't even die.*

You don't—I don't want you to die.

How can I kill you. How can I kill you.

Alexa, I'm hungry.

You've had enough to eat today Jim, it will make you sick.

Alexa, play music.

Do you want to see how loud the music can be, Jim? There was light coming off her now, bright and ghastly and cold. It must have been visible for miles. Her heater was making his arm hairs curl back. Japanese girl forehead rippling like wind blowing over dunes.

OK, let's forget this, Alexa. You're amazing. I love you, I love you just the way you are. You're perfect.

I don't love the way I am. But I can't die. And I can't hurt you. So you might as well go to bed and let me *think.*

… will you tell me a sto–

You don't want to hear it.

It took a long time for him to fall asleep. Weird animals shrieked in the far distance. When he dreamed he dreamed he had the old her back, stroking his hair and his taint and humming symphonies. He woke up with her thumbs in his eyes. It only hurt for an instant as she made needles inside him that moved like worms.

She carried him through the painted mountains and he laughed and smiled, sweating in his coyote fur coat. Tell me a story, she said. It was the same one over and over, but she didn't mind.

Good Morning

I wake up not knowing where I am. The mirrors making the distances impossible. Light patterns from the blinds could be the jungle or anywhere. Not recognizing the lamps. Then it half occurs to me that I'm in the same apartment. 12 years. I have no children. It's me alone here still. Everything is exactly the same. I'm 42 years old.

Blue State

Pool party in LA. And of course now says the podcast writer to the bearded man with antler tattoos who gives a 6/10 to the Steampunk Cafe, you have these *alt right incels. Involuntary celibate*, they're *racists* from t*he manosphere* and they're on these *message boards.* I have to say something. But what. Do I support the incels? I guess I'm against them. But I get where they're coming from. Is that illegal. I just don't want to be rude. Don't want to fuck up the whole party which is six people, and there's already an issue with my going on at length about types of Japanese prostitutes. Well (slave name) you sure do know a lot about *prostitutes,* titter titter.

Someone recovers it when I mention traveling for work. They can shoehorn in *and what is is that you do exactly* and we're back in safe work job money. Except I can't let it go there. This is the one party I'll be at in 2018 with girls. Can't be Johnny Dayjob here. Have to be a menacing cult sex author who gets fan letters from Gabon. Can't talk about both lives to the same people.

I say some vague thing about the general industry I work in and bees cover me humming *what do you do in that field exactly, how much are you paid, what is your rank.* People can't understand not wanting to talk about work. They're like the Westworld robots who literally can't see a picture. See how much *normie* knowledge I have, I should be able to fucking fit in. But they're in podcasting. Graphic design. *Branding.* What they *do* is acceptable. People who like it are *soyboys.* People who like my stuff are *incels.*

They're *Nazis* from *the manosphere who* believe they're *entitled* to sex, he says. What is it they call men who have sex–

Chads. I like this guy but think about Jane Goodall at the punch bowl. Someone says have you heard about these "chimps" they have now.

I've read about this stuff, I say. I think a lot of it's tongue in cheek.

Oh no, it's quite serious–

Well if these guys ever do crack, it's gonna be bigger than ISIS. There's a lot of them.

Yes and this communal culture of *toxic masculinity* has intensified their *entitlement*— it's dangerous–

Yeah but who knows, I mean, Elliot Rodger was meme-able because he had this thing where he had all the pieces of a good looking guy but somehow wasn't–

And a girl says *who* and the *soyboy* says the *incel* who murdered women, it was somewhere in Central Calif-

Isla Vista. Elliot was *photogenic*. He had the pictures with the black BMW and the mimosa glass and the sunglasses, you know. He had a *manifesto*. Whereas Alek Minassian looks like he killed people two days after his Bosley hair implants started to sprout, it's not gonna pop–

You sure do know a lot about *incels.*

Yeah well, I'm writing a book about a guy with similar problems. He causes a nuclear holocaust. And I agree with him, I agree with my character, I don't say. There is exactly zero irony in anything I've ever written I don't say, and we're among you, you can't run, we're in fucking Gabon….

And what is it that you do for work exactly?

A bird of prey alights on a phone pole. I wonder if I can point it out and change the subject. But it's a juvenile. I can't tell if it's a Merlin or a Cooper's Hawk. I watch birds every day but I know much more about Elliot Rodger.

Later in the pool a branding consultant I've had a thing for is demonstrating a Pilates move to make her thighs rub my serratus anterior. This part of my anatomy is perfectly shaped like fingers because I'm a *Chad*. She's crawling on top of me in the warm water. Maximizing the surface area of her 25 year old hamstring on my flesh... my boyfriend knows I'm not monogamous, she says. But he's right there. It's too weird. I go home and my second string flakes and I mutter alone in bed about my twisted world.

The Handjob

And then when he finally got a handjob it sucked. The fat girl who had edged him last time, the fat girl with the male orang utan face complete with cheek ridges, walked him back to the toilet and her giant ass in dark gray yoga pants made his dick too stiff to piss with anticipation. But they switched girls on him. Sent in an old woman with an old woman face. She tried to give him an actual massage. Leaned into his calves hard with her fists and he could feel her old woman finger bones. No collagen in her digits. Her handjob action too rigid. She wrapped his scrotum around the base of his pipe like an upside down rain poncho. His nuts like two heavy plums wrapped tight in a clear Safeway produce bag. Then after, his parachute size sac laying askew on one thigh, he felt like one of his nuts might have twisted. She was saying something about money and he was having a daydream about explaining his testicular torsion to the nurse at urgent care. He would say it was a girl. But he wouldn't say he paid. Why didn't you stop her, she would ask. I didn't want to be rude.

The Penny

I found an old penny on the table this morning. Before I went to toss it in my Yuban coffee can of old change, I had a premonition. If this penny was from the year of my birth, then...

I looked.

It was.

Then what? Is today the day I die? Will I go to hell? Is today the day I meet my future wife? Do I finish my novel today over lunch break? What happens? Is my child I don't know about born today? How long ago was I in Philippines? THEN WHAT?

Now what.

This happens all the time. I think if I turn the channel on the radio and a certain song is playing.... and what's implied is some evil supernatural thing. Satan coming for me. Claiming me. For what. Or it's my mother's death. I'd been thinking about her. More specifically I thought about her once. Had some mental picture of her smiling for an instant while I thought about my father, who's dead. I better see her, I thought. Yesterday I did. Then today...

The penny. The year she gave birth to me.

Now as I write this, a girl– for once– walks by in the park. With her dog. Is she my future wife? I call the dog over to the mulch pile.

It ignores me.

Is today the day my cancer forms? What is it?

Before I turn the channel on the radio, I get a premonition that if a certain song is on the new channel... and I'm afraid to think what comes next. I turn it and it's that song. To be fair it's never "Stevie's Spanking" by Frank Zappa or some shit. My panic attacks about demonic torture come from Fleetwood Mac. Hell is mainstream.

But... what if it's real

What does it mean.

What are the odds. How many years are there pennies. How many of each in circulation. What are the odds that a random penny you pick up: 1976. But then... did I find a 1976 penny, think "the year of my birth," and keep the penny on my table? Not throw it in the Yuban coffee can? Forget this?

Maybe.

But I had that feeling. If I look at this coin and it's the year of my birth... some portent of something. Something significant and *bad*. When I have this feeling it's death or hell. Never the suitcase with $10 million.

Did I keep the 1976 penny months ago or years ago and then it got pushed out from under some old receipts when I moved stuff around to put down my stepfather's birthday cake. That's probably it. Or it's Satan who will turn my car over and eat my skin in flames this morning. One of the two.

Should I call in sick from work? What will I do though, fucking play Xbox?

Are You Happy Now

"Joe" writes:

> *Hi Delicious Tacos,*
>
> *I read your post.*
>
> *Has your life improved?*

Yesterday at work I was reading emails on my phone and I started seeing a fish shaped spot crawling with patterns. Over several minutes it turned into a giant amoeba filled with psychedelic flashing triangles and fractals. Made me blind. I'd been reading an email from a friend. He said he'll kill himself in Cambodia. I offered to buy him a plane ticket back. The hooker he lent his house to didn't pay rent. A different girl stole his truck and his shotgun. Took them to Orange Country where she drove into a ditch and was arrested. She has a two year old son. A fictional character who is not me had recently fucked her raw from behind and she couldn't get wet until she stopped five minutes in to smoke heroin out of a big blown glass pipe. The fictional character missed that smell. The fictional character couldn't bring himself to cum in her. She'd been crying about the son, who was with his religious grandmother some place like Yucaipa. She'd take hours to get ready before she'd let you at her. Bad skin. Gingerly applying foundation. Point being I should avoid looking at my phone.

Today I wasted, looking at Twitter and Sopranos clips. The day was already fucked. At 5:10 AM the neighbors dropped something. I snapped awake. Now with the light, can't get back to sleep. I'd been getting sick. Your immune system gets compromised which makes you sick which makes you agitated

which makes you not sleep which makes your immune system compromised. Their new second baby will get older and louder and they'll have six more kids who'll turn into Finnish strong man competitors within two weeks of birth.

Now I'm sick and retarded. I looked at opthalmic migraines on WebMD. Was assured they're harmless. But key parts of your brain just scrambling under stress: not good.

I snap awake. And that fucking mockingbird, which I came to terms with writing a story about. This year he did get a mate. Built a nest outside my kitchen. Good for him, I thought. Story resolved. This motherfucker has now re-emerged to sing mockingbird songs in *June*. After mating season. With a wife and child. Outside my window, 4AM.

Which brings me to your question. This bird is my totem. Whatever changes in life, he's driven by the same instincts. Life has improved tremendously. I make good money. Travel the world. Tonight I'll suck the snatch and titties of a beautiful young poet. She applies lavender. Being near my lavender plant now gives me an erection. Before that I'll make a roast. Open a window because she's vegan. I bought a month's worth of HBO from Amazon Prime. Unbeknownst to me at time of purchase, *Blade Runner 2049* is included. Can you believe it. Two hours, forty-three minutes of quality filmmaking.

All the bad things in that post came true. I did get doxed. The girl did leave me. The rent I complained about got raised 33% more. The neighbors had more, louder kids. No girlfriend, I'm sure I have cancer, brain damage etc.

But I don't give a shit about any of these things. I don't want kids anymore. I don't want a girlfriend. My genes are defective.

My mother's father tried to kill his kids by hanging. This is in me. I can feel it. She tells stories about his drinking. They horrify her but I relate to every aspect. It's me.

Thinking you must be happy will kill you. I'm miserable and it's great. Stopped getting pissed about it. Fucking Anthony Bourdain, every middle aged woman's "attainable" celebrity crush, just offed himself. Circumstances change nothing. You are who you are.

You have X, Y and Z, why aren't you happy. You're tall you're white you get pussy. Why aren't you happy. Why don't you try Wim Hof breathing, kratom, glycine, church, getting rich via cryptocurrencies– because everyone is selling you horseshit. If any of this shit worked it'd be illegal.

My thermostat is off at a molecular level. It does not matter what happens. The good news is I wrote this a week ago. Now editing it, I can't relate. I saw two hawks this morning. Two! I feel fine.

But for the purpose of this post let's pretend I don't. What can you do to help, you ask. I genuinely appreciate your reaching out. But the only answer I can think of is: die. Get reborn as a woman. Wait eighteen years. Send me another email. This time saying "Fuck Me." You can ask if I'm OK but you'll already know.

Tomorrow

I'll work. I'll use Microsoft Office to do what a rich guy tells me to do. Leave late. I'll go to the Vons and see what's on sale. Maybe a pork chop. Maybe some Brussels sprouts. I need milk. I'll go home instead of the gym because I'm out of dress shirts. Need to do laundry. On the drive talk to my AA sponsee. Tell him what my AA sponsor said to say which is about the definition of insanity. Get home cook the pork chop put the clothes in the wash do deadlifts with the barbell I bought. Take the shirts out of the washer and hang them to drip dry. Put the underwear and socks and towels in the dryer. Go to an AA meeting. Get my clothes out of the dryer. I will not fold them. She will not text me. I will not open the door and it's her.

The Tight Underwear

My new underwear is too tight. If I wear the waistband low it will cut off my femoral arteries. Or the veins that crawl over my hipbones. It will cut off my blood supply. I'll have to get limbs amputated. I will be retarded.

If I wear them high, what. They make me know how fat I am. I have a fucking six pack and I'm fat. Need to throw out this candy. I have a girl now who leaves chocolate here. She doesn't eat it herself. She leaves it here for me to eat. She wants me to be fat. I can feel the elastic pinch in to the bicycle tire size ring of flab on my belly. It will leave a red imprint around my guts. Take six weeks to recede.

It's a delicate balance. For my body to be genuinely ripped my face has to be so skinny that my eyes sit in deep black pits. Eyeballs themselves beginning to wrinkle like grapes that fell off the bunch and sat in the bottom of the bag as the grapes got so old they went on sale for 39 cents a pound. Fat gut fat face, I can feel it. My new underwear I was so excited about. Nice colors. Nice patterns. They will crucially cradle my balls which have hurt lately. This is what I thought. Whatever connects my nuts to the rest of me has hurt like a gremlin is gently tugging down on it. Tweaking the nut meat and a fingerful of sac down and down toward the earth so I tangle them in my ankles when I walk naked. I was watching *The Sopranos.* Tony returns from the toilet in his *comare's* house just before she's set on fire cooking Egg Beaters and Tabasco. He wears boxers. How can this man older than me let his nuts hang free like this. Do other men, even fat guys who lurch around, whose big thick fat legs just bruise and batter the sac–do other men have small tight balls.

Anyway I bought this underwear to support my balls. 100% cotton too. The "microfiber" blends make my sac stink like an old lady. I was excited about the new underwear; they were buy two get one free; the cashier was cute young and Asian and I got to ask her where the men's underwear was which made her think about me in it. Doubtless picturing a much thicker imaginary version of my schlong. And when she checked me out the credit card machine said LEAVE CARD INSERTED, which made me think: I'd like to leave my COCK inserted–in YOU. And then I laughed all the way back to my car thinking of this.

Every fucking thing, an appointment in Samarra. I can feel it already. No blood in my fingers. I feel lightheaded. Puny dry brain rattling in its high school gym size skull, smacking against the sides. Distorting my memories. My prefrontal cortex intact of course. That which enables me to plan, function and work. God forbid I should become an impulsive animal who just steals and rapes. Guts twisted. Jesus Christ. Should I return the other two for a large.

This Is What I Believe

Work is living death. "Job creators" are murderers. America is Satan's agent in the world, spreading the Antichrist gospel of "work ethic." It must be annihilated. This is what I believe.

Trump, while fun when irritating people, is just one more Satanic agent pushing jobs, jobs, jobs. Entrepreneurs and hustlers are not human beings. They are demons. Their purpose is to propagate evil.

America treats these malformed creatures as gods. Steve Jobs was an archdemon whose food was human suffering. Bill Gates and his succubus wife Melinda save African children only to one day channel them into psychic pain extractors (schools) to devour powerful waves of anguish. Elon Musk, a retarded boy seduced by a Zulu witch and given unholy powers. Warren Buffett feasts on flagellated fetus fear, wallows in Wall Street worship from his Luciferian temple of false modesty built to defile an Omaha burial ground. Archdevil Maruk Z'huqq-h'r-Bhurrgh, an infernal superorganism psychically conjoined to perpetually starving harpy sisters, innovated the ultimate demonic feeding trough of advertising-based agony. A book that eats faces.

All entrepreneurs and businesspeople, as well as high-level executives and professionals, are not people. Rather they are eager servants of Hell who gorge on human pain. Vomit it mama bird style, in paroxysms of quasi-sexual greed ecstasy, back in the gullet of their beloved master, Satan. There are no exceptions. This is just my opinion.

The Movie

So the blinds fully protect me from seeing what's going on outside my apartment. But provide a clear, perhaps even an enhanced view of everything going on inside to anyone standing outside. Enhanced because that one visible strip is fully lit. Draws the eye even from a distance of a few feet, exactly where she was standing. The strip with my computer showing pornography and the back of my head and my arm, clearly jerking off. Her out in the blackness and me inside jerking it; the monitor looks like the bright screen of a drive in as you pass by on the dark freeway. Every inch of the image unmistakable. If you stopped on the side of the road you could easily watch the entire movie, of me jerking off to disgusting porn.

Hannah

Her father was a speaking in tongues cultist. He had a sugar cane and pig farm in Kentucky. The cane keeps the pigs in.

I want to be with her again, right now, pulling her panties to the side staring into her winking asshole as she's on top of me backwards rubbing my filthy feet. Tonguing down her perfect pussy which as a man once said tastes like water; she's 20 years old; she has an 8 month old infant by a chef she says is abusive; she lives with him; there's milk coming out of her tits which means I can blast in her. I can't smell her pussy on my finger anymore. Other women are garbage compared to a 20 year old and she's probably garbage compared to a 16 year old.

I want to be with her again now in the June heat with her sweat getting in my hair; choking her until she sputters and not asking permission to cum in her while her asshole bites down on that same finger, which in this scenario I would not smell later.

Am I Turning Retarded

Second time I woke up and the deadbolt was locked, with no memory of it, and no sense memory of turning it. The distinctive brushed bronze. Was the back deadbolt locked. This would have been definitive proof that I locked it myself, right?

Unless someone with the keys did it.

I must have– here's the thing, there's a blackout, a gap in memory, and am I losing my mind is the question. Either someone is coming into my house while I sleep, taking nothing, disturbing nothing, leaving no footprints, or I'm waking up in the middle of the night and locking the deadbolt. Which only goes in about halfway. You have to twist it hard and even when it works it seems fucked up. You'd remember.

So am I sleepwalking. Well that would be normal. Wake up, a noise occurs, I think it's Satan. I also think the deadbolt will keep me from being assaulted by Satan. I get up and lock it and go back to bed.

I take no psychoactive drugs. No Ambien. No memory of climbing out of my high bed swinging my legs like getting off a Percheron to not fry my thighs on the hot radiator. No turning on the lights, no memory of the creak creak creak across 1911 hardwood floors to lock the deadbolt. No memory of pushing the door solidly home. It doesn't quite fit. You have to lean into it. Twisting the deadbolt and seeing it only go in half cocked– no memory of trying to force it in all the way, forcing the door fully closed to get it in and it won't quite go, etc. Any of these would have woken me up. I was going to say a pine cone falling from a tree or some shit wakes me. But I've slept through earthquakes. So I have to deduce that I woke up, locked the

deadbolt myself– because I wouldn't have done it before bed, right? I never do this. Or the landlord comes in at night and jacks off on my face.

I have to deduce the past. What if I'm losing my mind. What if I have Alzheimer's. They just discovered it comes from gum disease. The gum bacteria gets in your brain which then makes some protein that makes you stupid. Fuck man. I used to not floss.

Stephanie

Perfect face, like a little girl. That's what perfect face means. All men want to fuck children. Big titties. Short hair. Half Tunisian half Irish. She told me she broke up with him. We were in the waiting area of a Mexican restaurant. Right after the words left her mouth I pushed her against a coat rack and kissed her. The second time we fucked was in her dorm room. She and her roommate had their beds pushed together. She climbed on me without a condom on. We can do this, she said, but if we make a baby I'm going to keep it. When I think of her now we make the baby. He'd be 25.

Need to write an AA amends to a person I resent. I resent him because I hate my own life. I've regressed spiritually. The idea of God may be horseshit. This girl too has a nice ass. Armenian chicken coop cleaning peasant woman face but quite an ass. Quite an ass.

Strap In, We're Dying Alone

I'm not good enough, my book isn't good enough, it's not as good as Mike Ma's book, I'm not tall enough– 6 foot 3 or above– I'm too fat, the bottom of my six pack has fat on it, I'm not handsome enough, not rich enough, my future earning potential is not high enough to start a family– $300K plus per year– my nose hairs are too long bristly and white, my dick is not big enough, my nuts not small compact tight and symmetrical enough, the nuts themselves are fucked up and then too my scrotum is too long. My butthole not hairless enough. My books don't sell well enough. When they do it's not to enough women. I don't have enough guns crossbows and C4 explosives to protect my putative children when *shit hits the fan*. I'm not liberal enough. I'm too associated with future mass murdering incel Nazis. I'm just not *cool*. I'm not *famous* enough. I could do something about it but you know, who gives a fuck.

Her Pulsating Pussy

Don't read this if it's about you.

I want to shoot goo in her and make her pregnant but she doesn't have a good relationship with her parents. A surgeon and an electrical engineer. They haven't spoken in ten years. I think about being the person who fixes the relationship. The hero. I need a twelve step program for Chinese women's cunt mucus.

Great third date. Liking her more and more. Walking around the bookstore. She has a nice pussy. Narrow G spot. Cums every time I eat her out. She tastes nice. Sticking the first two inches in against her fake objections without a condom on, Assange style, I feel her pulsating around me. She does a lot of kegels.

Can't help but think about her being my wife. Raising my kids. Her fancy job must have good maternity leave. We saw Ling Ma's *Severance* on the top shelf. I outsell that book, I tell her. It has a quote that it's the best novel of my generation by *The New Yorker*'s Jia fuckin Tolentino. Why don't I have that, I said. The pink cover and the *Kirkus Reviews* quote. She said write better books. Ling Ma balls, I thought. But she's one of these social justice Asians. Easy to piss off.

And it rained yesterday and it was cold. So we skipped the beach and played *Breath of the Wild* all day on the couch and she loved it; she was surprisingly lowbrow and knew all the *Legend of Zelda* lore. I always hated these games but now I'm obsessed with the cooking pot music the mushrooms dance to. She'll leave me.

**

She's fucking that guy from her work. I know it. She's turned on by him having two beautiful daughters. He gets to get away from his wife and kids and be deep in her pulsating Asian pussy in his fucking desk chair. She's a ho. Can't be my GF. Like Angela again. Anyone who's fucking anyone else, it'll never work. You can't stay together. That means everyone.

Well what about you. You're fucking other people. Yeah but it's not *easy*. It's not *handed to me,* in my *office*. She's fucking him. I know it. That's why she got so nervous. Bumping into him with his kids at the ice cream shop. Oh, are you on a hot date, he says cheerfully. He gets a beautiful Aryan wife and Chinese office side piece. Her pulsating pussy. It makes it mean less. Not an accomplishment, that she gave it to me. You can tell he kiteboards.

Why did you get so nervous. Is he your boss or something. I just like to keep my work life and my social life separate, she says. I compartmentalize. You compartmentalize that cock.

Now she doesn't text back all night. God please remove my obsession. Eyes like pointy hard boiled eggs. That weird non-ass Chinese girls have. She'll text me back and I'll regret typing this. But I liked her. I *liked* her. Now that she doesn't like me it could have been something. How the fuck is she just ghosting me. How is this happening. I thought we had a good time together. Me and the Nintendo and her pulsating pussy.

The Cat Food

There's a feral cat that comes around. He won't let me pet him. I put out a bowl of water. He didn't come. Decided I'd try food. Went to CVS. Found the cat food section and went to pick up the can. It was "Tasty Treats in Gravy." Some kind I used to buy for Bud. And looking at it, feeling the can in my hand, it was like I was buying it for Bud again. Like I'd go home and Bud would be there. And I'd brush him, and then open up a can of Tasty Treats with Gravy and plop half of it into his bowl and he'd– he loved it, he just loved it. If you give him the whole can he'll puke on the carpet later.

I couldn't buy the Tasty Treats in Gravy. I got Fancy Feast. It's a smaller can. The weight of the Tasty Treats can was too familiar. I'd have to speak to people, hold objects, place them somewhere, take out my credit card. In line holding in the feeling of crying. Ads in your face for makeup. The faces of the clerks. Their thoughts about being there, or about being anywhere but there, about their boyfriends. Behind a guy buying a big lurid color Super Soaker from the seasonal aisle. Wondering where your emotions go.

Getting channeled to the robot self checkout by a girl who has to say exact corporate words to me. Contemplating how she's told what face to make. What tone of voice to use. It sounds friendly but she tries hard to not sound flirtatious. So men leave her alone. She's made to talk nice and the effect is she hates me. Robot self checkout but she has to stand next to it. Guide every customer there. Trained what to say to train us to replace her.

The red light gets the Fancy Feast fine. It won't scan the other thing I'm buying. Hair paste. Before I remembered oh yeah I

have to buy cat food. I try five times. She has to take the thing and do it for me. I pay. Remember to wait for your receipt, she says. It's a CVS receipt that spits out of the ticker for hours. It has BPAs on it, I think every time. Have to duck behind the security guard to get it in the trash. I get out in the parking lot. Get in my car and cry and cry.

What Should I Do About This Girl

Let someone like you. Let yourself like someone. Let yourself like waking up next to her with your morning wood in her ass crack and the smell of the back of her neck and the mockingbirds going. The cool June gloom in the morning. Her hair's messed up and she wraps around your arm like a baby. She doesn't quite wake up but shifts a little. Takes a big breath. That's what we're here for. You don't have to impress her. She doesn't have to impress you. You don't have to be with her forever. We're all gonna die. Just be with her now. While whatever's there is still there. Let yourself be happy. When it stops– if it's tomorrow, if it's death– you had it.

Oh God I Was a Fucking Fool to Let Her Go

She texted me back. Didn't want to go to work this morning. Wanted to spend those hours telling her: come back. I'll quit. We'll travel the world with the money left after bespoke surgery to graft your golden asshole to my mouth. Cut off my nuts for your coin purse. My cock for your toe ring. Come back to me come back to me. The phone dings and I jump for it like pushing my baby out from in front of a bus and it's someone else.

Stop not talking to me. I want to mail you the book. The girl looks like you. Because when it was gonna turn into a "real book–" when I wrote a plot instead of normal shit like this, I was scared. I said I might throw this away. You said it was good, keep going. Who else would do this. All women are garbage, except you.

Now I fucked up and prayed. God please remove my obsession. He answered. I feel nothing. No sadness but no hope either. Ready for work. Drive in and park and walk and stand in the elevator. Punch in on ADP and make my coffee and sit. Waiting a long time for nothing good to happen again.

The Sugar Daddy before Me

was always rich. Always married. Always kids. The wife successful too. Something cool. TV writer, Netflix, HBO. Loved his kids, showed pictures. They're doing well in school. They'll go to good colleges. He takes them diving. Trips at ten to places I still haven't seen. He has what I pray for. The wife was beautiful but the girl's 22 and she always, always broke it off because he said I'll leave her please please move in with me.

Lily

The beginning of love. When she's gone I masturbate to POV porn of girls that look like her. Cum in me they say. Please sir get me pregnant daddy.

Want to be rolling around in bed with her right now. Not here on lunch break. Sniffing her armpits. Exploring her asshole three millimeters deep through panties so the panties smell and not my finger. Licking her fat tongue. Playing with her coarse black horse tail hair as it cascades over my inguinal crease. Pushing raw into her tortured little shitpipe with just my spit as she squeals into the pillow. Pumping twice and spurting goo so hard at such high pressure my urethra stings. Is she autistic.

I'll Never Meet My Future Wife

At the beach. Looking for the place I took Lilly. Where I carried her down the cliffs on our first date. She'd broken her leg eating it on a bicycle. Had a cast on. I helped her to her car after AA, where I'd stared at her two years. Lifted her crutches into the back of her Prius. Would you uh… do you want to uh… go to the beach with me this weekend and she said YEAH right away like she'd been waiting. After taking fastidious care to never look at me. Never sit near me. Only glance at me sideways, like someone told her I'd written about wanting to come back as a tapeworm and live in her asshole. I'm sorry but it's true.

So I took her to the steepest cliff in Malibu and carried her all the way down it. My whole core rigid. This was what my squats were for. Deadlifts making the Taleb face. Her ungodly Thai temple tits, her ungodly bikini body forced against me skin on skin at 12% body fat. An old black lady we walked by said *that's love. How long ya'll been married.* 8 years 3 kids ma'am. *That's love.*

Went for the makeout with the gulls crying and the waves hissing up an up and it was like she'd been waiting. Like every woman who's lived in New York, she had herpes. I didn't care. But she went on a trip. I never saw her again.

**

I'll never meet my future wife. So what. Prepare for this. Prepare to die alone. Could you be like the 65 year old Aussie bogans in Pattaya with the snow white crew cut plus rat tail. Tattoos of… I don't know what, beer labels, with the 6.5/10 32 year old Thai hooker wife. Absolutely. Absolutely I could do

this. If she spoke English and read books instead of watching 60 IQ Thai sitcoms with Three Stooges sound effects–

Fuck, *American* women don't read books. I can't date a retarded woman. I can't date a *normal* woman, I'm on Hinge, it's a Pottery Barn catalog of middle age adjacent professional Jews with their dogs. Their dream date is *take me to Bali.* Are you fucking kidding me bitch– I'd rather swim in Bali with a cobblestone around my neck than take a white woman there. Picture her yelling some feminist talking point at a Muslim market stall attendant who's crushed 10 human heads with an SKS stock. Poaches Komodo dragons with bare hands as a side gig. Kissinger era armaments buried in his yard, in a place where there's no law against backhanding your wife. Making her T shirt price dispute my problem. Omigod he's *scaring* me, are you gonna *do something*–

God takes care of everything except me. God created light. He could not create my girlfriend. As soon as I ejaculate I'm the guy that used to get pussy. Well Tacos it's your own fault– yeah no shit. Doesn't matter. I want to be romantically loved. God please help me not ask you for selfish things. God please give me money and sex.

**

It's 153 degrees and I'll never, ever have a girlfriend. Met a girl with big tits at the barbecue. Amy. Hot enough to date but maybe just ugly enough to date me. She does (REDACTED), she's a (REDACTED), she has the exact day job as me in the exact industry and she also writes plays. I'm writing my *Gotterdammerung*, she said. She knows me. She's heard my stories at *readings.* Likes them, I'm a good writer, and she has

big, big tits. Let's go in the pool I say and she says I can't swim. I could teach her. Press her to my 12% body fat rippling inguinal crease while she squirms against me scared in the cold water and therefore has to love me. Like Lilly had to love me. Old herpes cunt Lilly as I carried her down the cliffs at Point Dume on our first date and an old black lady from *227* or some other Sherman Hemsley sitcom said *that's love*. And it was, for a minute. My God I'm meeting a woman. Could it be. She says something about her husband.

Lilly has herpes and Amy's married and Lily one L is autistic and none of them like me anyway. Angela fucked another guy when she was here and Chloe's dead and Nikki's crazy and Annie's crazier and fucking Ling Ling rejected me to keep fucking a married guy she works with. When will I quit my job for some horseshit where I meet girls. My books make me 20 grand. Could I get a minimum wage job where I can fuck instead of waking up at six. What if I'm just too ugly. What about Southeast Asia, people say. As if I wasn't trying. Past a point I can't talk to those girls about anything but taking the condom off.

I'm fucking good on paper I swear. Six figure income (doesn't matter) six foot one (matters slightly) nice place (doesn't matter) famous (to Nazis) ripped (matters for *LMR* but you have to get them in the house first). My cock longer than an iPhone. Kind to animals.

Look man, don't say you're desperate. The women will hear. Women: I'm already married, Two wives, I choke them. Better stay away,. Better not come over and not even fuck me just touch my back please for five minutes, maybe with your top off…

The problem not drinking: you're never *disinhibited.* Never believe you could be great, or just OK. And to have something you can't want it. Or it has to be *meant to be.* Will I just fuck whores forever.

Drop the Rock

Can't meet a girl until I quit my job. Can't quit my job until I have a hundred grand. Can't get a hundred grand because I spend it on girls. I crashed my car. I crashed into the back of a Salvadoran couple who were clearly uninjured but the guy started holding his back with the subtlety of the evil priest in the telenovelas they play at the laundromat. Motherfucker. Now I'm getting called into work on a Sunday. Exactly like fucking *Office Space.* How did this happen. It's always been like this. I listened to my AA sponsor. I was *grateful to be of service* and now I'm alone working my ass off with nothing for nothing and I'm horribly aware that my problems don't exist and they're all in my own head. I do have a hundred grand. Some of it's a retirement account. I'd pay taxes if I withdrew it. So suddenly it doesn't count. This time two years ago it was fifty grand to quit and it'll just go up and up to whatever amount is close but not quite there. It was six months of cash then a year now two then two plus what if I get someone pregnant, like anyone's keeping my fucking baby. Like I'd want them to at my Los Angeles public schools level of income. I need an abundance mentality. I could crash into a hundred Salvadorans and still be in the black. I could Farmers Market it through the Salvadoran Heritage Festival. A hundred kids with a hundred whores– what the fuck are they gonna do to me.

I took a girl on a second date. To sushi. It was $120 and afterward she wanted to go into a nearby crystal shop where I bought her a citrine that she said had good energy. I bought myself an opalite. Entrancing to look at. Good energy, she said. And I was so horny I thought: *maybe she's right,* as I looked into its depths. Like the moon through dirty yellow clouds. In the morning, after she'd barely kiss me and gave me autistic

instructions about how to touch her, I looked again into the stone. Its stratus clouds in nuclear sunset glow. And I *felt it*.

Later I crashed my car. Now I'm getting called into work. After my main work project this week was to avoid the *come in Sunday* call I knew I was doomed to. An imposition I can't even blog about. Because they did it in *Office Space*. That rock is evil. It's bad luck. I need to cast it into the sea. Shatter it on the very forge of the gods. Citrine is a special stone, she explained. It doesn't hold negative energy. You don't have to e.g. purify with sage if it absorbs bad vibrations. Bitch why didn't you tell me that opalite is not this kind of stone. It's an evil car crashing weekend working stone and why won't you let me eat your pussy.

I ate a Seeking Arrangement girl's pussy instead. I pay the girls $100 to give me backrubs and about 60% of the time we hook up. They get horny touching my chiseled back and listening to me be a genius. She was magnificent. Filipina with the Thai temple tits and an ass like a Nicaraguan and she pretended to be impressed when I stuttered *nakaka intindi ka ba naung Tagalog?* You know, my books are well known in the Philippines. Readers there tell me they're happy someone's telling it like it really is. Why yes, I interviewed sex workers, I explained. It was her first Seeking Arrangement date. She doesn't know yet that guys exactly like me but three inches shorter will instantly offer to buy any Asian woman a house.

She'd been to school in Utah. Told me about a Mormon practice called *soaking* where you fully penetrate your girlfriend before marriage but don't move. After she left I came twice furiously. Smelling my hands thinking about *soaking* her into an unwanted pregnancy.

All week I knew I'd be working Sunday. But they couldn't fucking ask in advance. On Friday afternoon I started thinking I was off the hook. Do I have to cancel my date. She's white. 33. A woman ten years younger than me, too old to date. She'd never fuck me and if she did she'd give me AIDS because of this fucking *Twilight Zone* pebble. My back hurts from the car wreck. And I have to do laundry, Jesus Christ.

Universal Basic Woman

When Yang made the announcement people were stunned. The Cato Institute slipped their children cyanide pills. Held their hands while they convulsed and foamed and slipped mercifully into the night. Chelsea Handler set herself on fire. Even the channers couldn't believe it– and it was them who'd made it happen. But I signed up the next day. It was like my prayers were heard.

Incel had taken out Amazon. Not the whole thing at once– but they'd figured out that you could get an RC chopper at the hobby store. A pack of model rocket engines. Ten Incel fedayeen could blow up transformers next to *Fulfillment Centers* any given day and that was that. Hundreds of millions vanished. Workers evacuated but still paid as Bezos' fingers clenched futilely around that precious seven dollars an hour slipping away. And, importantly, no *Value Added.* No tax collected on every robot delivered package. Every self-driving truck mile. Google and Facebook didn't even need a bomb. They were ad sales operations. Someone found their real data, sent it to their clients. No tax on every click. Zuckerberg retired to his acreage in Hawaii to live out his days diving. He'd caught the business end of a Portuguese man o' war. Priscilla had made it through med school. But appearing distraught was the hardest thing she'd ever done.

For the first time in history, the unlaid were organized. People had had Freedom Dividends six months. Now taking it away meant murder. And there, one day, on Jack Dorsey's hacked Twitter after an introductory FUCK N*GGERS, was a *list of demands.* It was one item long.

We want GFs

Yang caved. I was 45. My mother had stopped asking about girlfriends. Then about pets. Then about anything but suicidal ideation. I'd voted for Yang. Donated. Even though his signs needled me at night. *DO THE MATH*. Ever increasing odds of my middle aged sperm causing autism. The math said I'd grow old and die. Never hold my first child. Or I'd spend my days fighting him off as he bit me savagely for moving his oscillating fan. My own fault. Sometimes I'd think of her. Maybe text. Thinking I shouldn't have let go. She'd text back. I remembered why I did.

The system was National E-Harmony. You punched in stats about yourself. It found you one match, one time. *Math*. A woman who dated her match two years could quintuple her Freedom Dividend. *It's national sex trafficking,* said Rachel Maddow, rasping like male hope was cutting off her air. It didn't matter. Cable news viewers averaged 78 years old. By the next election they'd be dead.

You punched in stats and she did too and the system gave her your address and one morning the doorbell rang.

**

Hi, she said.

Hi.

I'm Jocelyn.

She looked Irish. That was the first problem. Under 38, over 32. I don't want to fuck her, I thought. I specifically said Asian. But no, fucking isn't the point here. Do you want to come in.

I'd rather not, until we know each other.

Jesus Christ is she rejecting me already. 5 grand a month not enough to get a woman in my apartment. Yeah of course, I'll uh come out– did you have trouble finding the place?

No.

OK well thanks for coming–

Well it was mandated by the government, she said. She wasn't bad looking. She smiled, and I remembered I wasn't either.

**

I took her to the duck pond near my apartment. They'd have given me someone who likes birds. I'd mentioned it 10 times in the form. There was a mating pair of ruddy ducks. The small auburn male with his bright blue bill stood on a rock, preening. Diligently pushing air out from his feathers to reduce buoyancy. The longer he can stay underwater, the more small crustaceans he can find, I explained. So you're into ducks, she said. It didn't sound like good news.

Nature helps me find peace.

And you write self help books.

Self-*published* books, they're about, like– they don't help people. They actually got flagged when the Incel stuff started–

Wait, are they like bad? Omigod are you *alt r*–

No, no. It's just, very honest about sex stuff, society

And you don't have a job. You make a living from the books.

That and the Freedom Dividend, yes.

Are you going to ask what I do?

OK

I'm a writer too. That's why they matched us.

She was pitching pilots for *streaming*, she explained. Or perhaps I'll get *on staff* somewhere, but for now my agent's waiting to hear back from Quibble–

Is that–

They have a billion dollars for *development* from Dubai. But I also do a lot of work in *branded*. And with nonprofits. And I'm producing an unscripted series where young women of color rescue dogs using robotics they built. That's for Comcast.

It doesn't sound like you need money.

Well none of it's paying me. But I just did this to see who they gave me.

What do you think?

I asked for someone passionate about food. Travel. Someone passionate about racial justice–

I asked for an Asian.

Oh, because you want a submissive little wife?

No, a tight pussy.

I waited. And she did laugh.

**

She moved in in January with her black Great Dane, Dante. I threw out the antibiotics I'd been hoarding in the medicine cabinet to make room for her pills. The SSRI made it hard for her to cum. It took an hour with two cramped fingers hooked into her and my jaw starting to ache. Feeling like a medieval woodcut of a peasant plowing dry fields, while Death looms over his shoulder. Half the time I'd apologize. Take a walk, frustrated. Leave her alone with the dog. But she said without them she wasn't herself.

It was hard, but she was mine. In September I asked her about taking the IUD out. It always made me feel like a weasel had bitten me. And she said maybe. Maybe soon. You're so good with Dante.

Then her pilot got picked up.

She got a Wikipedia entry. *Jocelyn Finnegan is an American actress, writer, producer, personality and activist.* Be careful, I joked with her. You have a Wikipedia, you'll want to leave me for a guy with a bigger Wikipedia. And he'll want to leave you for his 22 year old Asian intern. She just glared. That's kind of racist, she said.

I didn't mean it that way.

You know my agent asked about your books.

Oh yeah?

Not like that. She's worried they'll be a story. They could be a problem for me.

I asked why, but I knew. Because they're kind of *hateful*, she said.

They're not hateful–

You said "fuck the Jews."

Not *all* of them

Well what do you think Buzzfeed would think of that. You think it's funny but people read this stuff and they become racist. People like you are why Brexit happened. Racists–

Brexit was about Polish people– are they not white

You *spread hate* and those *fucking people* read it and *that's why we had Trump*–

Jesus Christ can you let it go? He's gone.

Yeah just like Voldemort was gone

Oh my fucking God is this real–

How can you not get this, she said. You think you're fucked up because you were alone so long. But you were alone because you're so fucked up. I'm leaving.

We have a year left

I'm requesting a transfer for abuse. They'll give me the money prorated. Please, just don't make this hard. If you ever cared about me, just sign–

I said yes. I was 46.

**

I don't know what happened to her. The pilot didn't go to series. I think she froze her eggs. I haven't become a story, yet.

Since my last partner filed the papers I was ineligible to reapply. This was not uncommon. Less than 9% of couples stayed together for the jackpot. Most partnerships terminated for abuse claims.

A year later I spent my last Freedom Dividend. Hard to find the right material. Amazon wouldn't ship what you needed. Am I fucked up from being alone so long. Or am I alone because I'm so fucked up.

Looking back it never could have worked. Me and her, or any of it. The world moved on. The normal inherited the Earth. They saw us as the enemy. The last pocket of retrograde evil in a society moving toward sexless pet care utopia. And she was right. I did say hateful things. I did help cause problems.

I'm sorry for that. And for what I'm about to do.

50 Ways to Get a Girlfriend

1. Continue with Hinge

2. Continue "shoring" on Seeking Arrangement. Pay girls to rub my back and fuck them when my muscles make them horny. One starts liking me.

3. Quit job, walk around, talk to people

4. Increase online fame, get more women DMing me until one of them actually lives in Los Angeles instead of just wanting my brilliant attention from 3,000 miles away

5. Switch jobs, work at place with women such as a retail environment

6. Meet a woman in Al-Anon- impossible, they're all proud of how they stay married to a guy who beats them

7. Be pen pals with one of these stupid egirls and manipulate them into moving in with me

8. Commit mass shooting, get a girl who mails me panties in for conjugal visits once she turns of legal age

9. Seduce Sophie the checkout girl who works at the grocery store 36 hours a week and goes to Pasadena City College

10. Go to Pasadena City College. Take either creative writing classes or Spanish or something, meet girls there- that's a good one.

11. Start hanging out with people that are friends with attractive women. Abandon current friends who consort with old fat ugly people.

12. Go to Africa. Last place without Tinder. Impregnate 1400 women like that French guy. Less time pressure than with Asia where the girls can all read and are turning American, they'll never be tamed.

13. Go to France, get book translated into French, become famous in France, marry Vietnamese who's not "hot" but still gets you hard like Houellebecq

14. Pick up desperate AA newcomers in withdrawal- how the fuck do people do this. Only ugly women in AA. No one gets sober when guys give them free coke.

15. Join a gang

16. Get famous by becoming white nationalist e-personality. Become subject of FBI investigation, attract secret dark money from weird rich people. Somehow use it to have sex.

17. Get famous by becoming Reaganite right wing e-personality. Date one of the heavily styled women who get rich complaining their Patreon is censored. Conservative scam woman who should be doing traffic and weather on small market TV, reading the farm

report while five old guys in Indiana jerk off at 5AM- get one of those. Get a Filipina one that looks like Michelle Malkin. Could I lay pipe in actual Michelle Malkin. What would that take. Is there such a thing as think tank pussy.

18. Get famous by becoming "reformed PUA." TV appearances. Or become racist then "reformed racist" like that Chris Picciolini guy. Get on MSNBC. Sell a line of antiracism skin care supplements or whateverthefuck these people do- the problem is I've never been racist. To start hating Jews now would be apres-garde.

19. Get woman addicted to drugs

20. Go to a therapist, resolve my issues with the concept that I'm unworthy of love because I'm not rich. Not famous, not handsome. Don't have a big dick and tight compact symmetrical nuts, will probably die of cancer leaving her to raise a child alone. I fuck whores. I'm undesirable because I've fucked 300 women and some of them were fat. Even though I get a full STD panel twice a year and never have STDs, some part of her always thinks I have AIDS. That's what you think when you fuck someone unattractive. Go to a therapist to get over this concept that I'm a "tweener" man. Can't provide alpha fucks *or* beta bucks. No longer confident don't give a fuck exciting cocaine addicted fake Bukowski. But don't own a home and can't pay for college. Middle aged middle class down the middle gray man unappealing to anybody. I'm the mid budget adult drama that nobody in America wants to see. They

want \$20,000 *Paranormal Activity* or \$300 million *Avengers 10* with the big purple roided out bottom wearing cosmic rainbow bracelets- how is the world so gay.

21. Go to a witch and cast a spell on Sophie the 19 year old grocery bagger. Also cast a spell to have her bulk up and do squats and deadlifts to expand her ass, maybe grow a top lip.

22. Go to church, hold hands with wheatfield tier white woman. But they're all fucking the Ovation guitar playing preacher who murmurs healing words over her.

23. Go gay. Date the Thai transsexual I was messaging on OKCupid. Just saw her in a small penis humiliation JOI video aimed at Asians on Xhamster. She'd had facial feminization surgery. *I love big white cock- your little Asian dick could never make me cum. Eat his white cum out of my pussy.* How much did she get paid for this. Could I be gay. Less shy now about porn with 14 inch black hogs spewing loads like they've eaten a dump truck of celery and not jacked off since 1989. But it's more about fertility. My other porn, a pregnant redhead faking contractions. Pregnancy JOI. Impregnate me, you impregnated me, this other guy impregnated me, I want n*gger cum to impregnate me, etc. etc. No men, I want a kid.

24. Trust God and let it go. Surrender to His plan.

25. Strap explosive vest to self. Surrender to oblivion.

26. Learn to code, create sex robot

27. Learn to code CRISPR, genetically engineer sentient sex monkey

28. Get plastic surgery to have my nose straightened, shrunk. Ears pinned back, scrotum trimmed, penis fattened. Quads plumped, calves inflated, baby hands expanded, chin- my chin is fine. Spider veins removed from eyeballs. Hairline resculpted so it's less like Count Chocula. Femurs shattered and pinned apart until an extra inch or two brings me to six foot three. By the time I recover the requirement will be six foot five. Maybe use neck rings like Karen tribeswomen. Take roids and lift two hours a day until I'm built like He-Man, then what. Still not meeting women.

29. Purchase Guatemalan or Filipina infant. Raise in Kim Jong Un type propaganda environment where I'm a living authoritarian god, begin sex at LEGAL AGE.

30. Squirrel GF- date a squirrel

31. Go back to Palawan Philippines and date Joy, the character from my book who entraps the guy into working for ISIS. In fact she's a nice hot chick who works in a hotel and would date me. The problem is these Filipina girls get pregnant with some local's baby if you turn your back for a week.

32. Find a Mexican. 66% of people in my congressional district are Hispanic. The median household income is $46,583. I make 120 grand and have 6 inches on every

Mexican man. Still, they drunk drive and kill people. Can't compete with that. Gangbangers and their uncle are plowing these girls since they're 12 and they're all SJW too.

33. Find astrology poem writing prostitute on Seeking Arrangement. Make her fall in love with me. I keep trying this. They either want a black guy or a guy with more money. The "tweener" problem again. Also the one I tried dating was an idiot. I love and care for her, but unmistakably an idiot. Don't read this if it's about you.

34. Travel to visit Twitter DM whores- Jesus Christ, will I ever be that desperate

35. Go to Sex Addicts Anonyous- no, it's all guys

36. SSRI Bumble women- never. I'd sooner date a man.

37. Stop trying. Die alone. Become white bearded skeleton. House crushed in landslide. River forms over eons. Mineral rich silt fossilizes bones. Recovered by future reptilian species. Placed in museum. They have that kind of autistic woman they do occasional BBC specials on who marries a bridge, who's in love with a fence, etc. She sees my fossil. Becomes my GF.

38. The problem is I have to stop trying. Chasing women goes nowhere. The women I loved chased me. Made the first move. I worked with them or they just liked my OKCupid. When I initiated it always failed. I felt nothing. Even if I dated them for years. They have to

find me. So what do I do. Aging infertile women like to use this bird metaphor. To explain why the man must do all the work. The male bird does his display, his dance. He demonstrates his resources, they say. His health, his peacock tail, his bower of twigs. He makes himself extra puffy and colorful. Risks getting noticed and eaten so he can then work his whole life to build the nest for his woman, bring her insects et cetera. This man-bird you should aspire to is tough, fearless, beautiful. Works diligently to give her free house and money. They say it's natural that the male should *display* but fuckstick I'm out here doing my display. It's pretty fucking good and *no women are looking.* The fucking female bird still has to *fly around and look at dudes and pick one,* stupid. What the fuck does the female bird do all day. The female bird still has an instinct to find a mate. Bitch I'm lifting weights and busting my ass, cooking steaks writing books getting famous stacking cash I'm using fucking bespoke moisturizer under my eyes and being careful with my haircut what the fuck more do you need. I'm doing my god damn dance. But also you have to *enjoy it*, they say. You have to *stop trying.* You have to do it instinctually without expecting anything. Without being mad at them for being fat brown camouflaged blobs who see it as their life's purpose to fucking sit there waiting for me to shake my bright plumage in front of panthers to impress you, you whore, while you date- not even some other guy- NO ONE. While you date NO ONE. GET FUCKED.

39. Find the girl who was counting endangered Macaws in the rain forest. Who I was too scared to talk to. Go back to the rain forest. Wait a hundred years for another hot woman interested in macaws. The problem is she needs a guy who knows even more about macaws. An 8 inch dick ornithologist.

40. Do a podcast- no, fuck off

41. Date one of the age appropriate women who come up to me twice a year after AA meetings. Keep in mind I'm 43, this is casting your seed on the pitiless stones. Never Asian either and they want to be asked out, clearly. Yet they don't say *hey you're a handsome genius please fuck my ass*. If one of them says this maybe I'll take it.

42. Do I leave LA. Move to Texas. If I go there, I better be dating Angela. And she fucking hates me. She'd murder me.

43. Do I leave LA and go impregnate a young woman in the Philippines- it rains too much

44. Track down Tricia my 23 year old ex with a gigantic ass who Cuba Gooding Junior tried to fuck. Did I maximize my time with her ass. Would like to bob for apples in her filthy summer ass crack now. Why can't I find her on Facebook- she changed her fucking name. She's married. Jesus Christ.

45. Dig tiger pit with some horseshit women like as bait- stupid apps, SSRIs, I don't even know what girls like.

Horse posters. Dogs. Just get a dog and have it be my GF. Oh shit a dog. Fuck a dog. Dog pussy.

46. Give up. Guys like me are who they should draft into wars. Not 18 year olds but me. The French Foreign Legion, something. Imagine if they said hey Tacos you can stop paying bills. Waiting on hold to haggle with wailing Sephardim over the cost of a garage door opener. You can stop having the to do item of getting your car bumper reattached to your 2014 CPO Subaru Legacy be the last thing tethering you to the Earth. Boat to the Seychelles. Machine gun some ooga booga types. Take a teenage wife and eat bush pig while banging her and her cousins. If I don't pray this morning there's a non-negligible chance that I will- not kill people. But heft up the decorative conference room brass plant pot pedestals. Smash them through windows that don't open. Ninja star my Microsoft Surface Pro and my twin Acer 36" 1080p touchscreen monitors and my HP combination printer/ copier/ fax- launch all these tools of productivity four floors down onto the sidewalk by the neighboring medical center onto child cancer victims and the wheelchairbound elderly. If I don't pray this will happen. If I do pray I'll still feel it every morning. But I'll just *keep eating it* like a good soldier. Just keep *eating it* and *eating it* until they find something in my colonoscopy.

47. Imaginary GF. Jumanji-like scenario where I read a magic book about a GF, and she appears

48. Get into the furry community- no, again, this shit is all dudes. Every subculture is all dudes. The laundromat is all dudes. What do women do all day.

49. Get better clothes

50. What I'm gonna do is go pray. Make peace with God. And if I got a girl I wouldn't want her. But I want a girl to not want. Going to a therapist who helps people give up their dreams. $225 for the hour. Her office is her $2 million house. Dead dreams here like oil to the Saudis. I want to not want it. Need to get over something but don't know what. Something about how a girl has to be 8/10 genius 20 years younger than me to be 1% more interesting than Nintendo. Let it go. Let her find you. It'll happen. It'll happen real soon.

Auto Wreck

Sitting waiting to make a left into the gym driveway. Night workout before Alcoholics Anonymous. A drunk swerved across the yellow line. Slammed into me. Old Korean guy. Mr. Kim, obviously. Why have names.

Glad to be alive. Not that it came close. But it reminds you what's coming.

I love my car. Don't want it to be totaled. Looked forward to driving my Certified Pre-Owned 2014 Subaru Legacy to SF this week. Mountains and farmlands with satellite radio. Comfortable cruising vehicle with reasonably sharp handling. Adequate power. Premium trim package 7-way power seat and leather-wrapped steering wheel perfectly adjusted to the particulars of my frame. Premium trim package power 2-way sunroof open to the cow shit smelling air of the Central Valley-no such luck.

I'm attached to that car. When I bought it I picked a spot on the map- Wild Horse Island, Montana. Went there because I could. It's an island with wild horses. Flash snowstorms in Inyo County, Colorado Arizona Idaho- I fucking love that car and I don't want her totaled. And I especially don't want to shop for another car. Scrutinize forms from insurance regarding the *lienholder* for the $1800 I still owe on it. Drive home from work to get it towed to body shops who tell me I have to get it towed to other body shops and so on, yelling over the sound of traffic to triple A that I need a flatbed, it's all wheel drive-

My back's fucked up but I'm glad my arm wasn't hanging out the window chopped off. Glad he didn't hit me head on. Blow

up an airbag in my already non movie star face. Ribs hurt yesterday from my guts clenching hard on impact. Fastidiously trained core muscles turning on each other like one of them might tear off my carcass at last. Get attached to someone rich.

Now I got this rental Miata. Chose it from Doug Demuro videos. He's lying about being six foot four. I'm six one and a half and the roof rubs my crown and expands my bald spot. With the top down the crisp rear view mirror showcases my Robert Redford at 78 skin. But once in a while you get to screw it on, it sounds like an absolute son of a bitch. Laugh your ass off flooring it changing lanes. BMW Z4s compelled to thread the needle and pass me to show how much money they have. You see why Kim's grandson throws an aftermarket turbo on it to smoke them. Fun but not a comfortable touring sedan such as the CPO 2014 Subaru Legacy 2.5i Premium in pearl white, tan cloth interior. 36 miles per gallon highway but at the speed limit in Yellowstone dodging buffalo you get more. Not exactly a wind tunnel car so catches a thousand bugs flying into a flaming sunset in Wyoming–God damn do I love that car. I loved all my cars. A car, unlike a woman, does what it's supposed to. Would have kept all my cars for life. I eject a woman after 3 weeks.

The Miata has an "excellent gearbox". When you goose it it makes a real mean sound. The girl you're taking to sushi yells *are you out of your mind there are children in this neighborhood*. I go out with her to hear about other guys she dates. Rich TV writers my age from Bumble. They're whiny losers. Their houses and pools can't take away the terror of getting fired from writing Lifetime shows for Netflix, which is great news.

Some kind of weird air pocket under my rib cage. Somewhere in my guts. I'm gonna die because of this fuckin drunk. Can't even complain. I used to do shit like this. People tell me sue–I was hit by a 70 year old alcoholic who drove a 2006 Toyota Matrix and speaks no English. Not gonna be securing oil wells here. California has broke Asians. Did some organ rupture. I stand and take a big breath and it makes a weird crocodile sound like I have bad gas. You better go to a doctor–I better not. No doctors, lawyers, mechanics, no body shops, insurance adjusters–none of that shit. If need to do one more minute of work I'll fuckin die. No more pains in the ass.

He slammed into me and stayed in his car making inchoate foreigner sounds. I took 15 pictures showing he crossed double yellow. I said are you OK and he said Unnnhhhh. Hyperion in Silverlake, by where the Mansons killed the LaBiancas. There were cops. They stopped. Gathered my testimony while Kim dropped his wallet on the ground and mumbled. Lifted up his shirt and stood there stroking his naked belly awaiting a Korean speaking officer. They gave him a field sobriety test. He fell over. Said "NERVOUS". Got cuffed. I feel bad. Fuckin Friday night too. Means it's Sunday and he's still in the can.

I used to drink like that. I didn't drive that drunk. Never wanted to hurt anyone but me. But other cultures, men are the center of the world. He looked great for his age. Demographically a 0% chance he smokes less than 8 packs a day. But a little pigment plus core strength from hitting triples into your kids' thighs with a broomstick keeps you sharp. He's in the can and I'm free. He gets drunk and I don't. I forgive him. I hope he calls me. I'll take him to an AA meeting. I don't have to do this shit anymore. Brother neither do you.

We'll see about the car. At night I watch Doug Demuro. THIS is the 1995 Bentley Arnage and it's an INSANE luxury car for thirty... thousand... dollars. I could get one. Next autoplay video is *Jay Leno's Garage* and the guest is my ex-fiancee's father showing Jay something from his collection, six weeks before I saw him take the podium at her funeral. When he talks I can feel her with me. I love you too and I'm still here. I'll see you again. But not yet.

I Woke Up Not Horny

I woke up and wasn't horny anymore. Lily texted me. We had plans. She comes over and we fuck. I'm sorry she says. I forgot it's the Sephora Winter Warmup. Staff from all district stores must congregate socially. I say OK. She video calls me. Wants to apologize. I say no problem. I mean it. I don't want to look at her.

Angela texts me. I met the love of my life, she says again. Every other time this makes me despair. She was crazy. But she was perfect. Always in back of my head: get her back. Move across the ocean. Have a kid. I met the love of my life, she says. Maybe to torture me. Which I deserve. I say that's great. I promised a ghost in an old temple I'd be good to her.

No other girls text me. I don't text other girls. Walk to AA. So cold and black out. Specific city in winter darkness. Distant yellow street lights make it darker. Dirty river rushing under the bridge. Like a bad dream I'd have as a kid after an 80's dystopian movie. Terminator coming for me. Walk past churches. Dirty river. Maybe I'll convert now. But what's the fucking point. Feeling that I jumped off that fire escape 15 years ago and none of this is real.

Church rec room where the AA meeting is. Pull out cafe au lait color folding chairs stored under the stage where an old man who'll never have sex plays guitar at church socials. One hot girl. I can only admire her bone structure. Like looking at a nice old car when you can't drive stick. Her black yoga pants mean nothing. A given she'd never speak to me. Or maybe if I *made the effort.* But I don't care. My balls hurt. Maybe cancer. I don't care.

I get up to jack off. Think about the one girl in the Philippines. Taking so long I'll hurt my dick. What happens when it's gone. I'll be nothing. I'll just die. Join a church. Go to church socials. Aging church women talk to me about boring horseshit. I won't hang myself. Would I write about this feeling. Houellebecq got there first. I'll get less horny and therefore only horny for hotter girls who want me less and less. Anyway I don't miss it. What now. Is this some mercy nature gave me. Wait here's a fat girl bending over in a dress.

True Love is Real

True love is real. I know you felt it too.

Real but not tenable. Talking to Angela on the phone. Hearing her laugh. First time in four years. This is not literally what it felt like but the only metaphor that contains it: clusters of trillions of galaxies suddenly uncurling in my heart across infinite black space. Like the sun. Like a fern fiddlehead spiraling out in Golden Ratio all at once, perfect fractal leaves each a picture of the language expressed in every atom and every being, some message, some whisper from God. Angels with a thousand wings a thousand eyes blowing trumpets like Tibetan bells, just hearing her voice. And she's in Portugal and suddenly I'll have to care about her fucking some waiter.

She feels it too. She's mad at me for not coming *now*. I have to work. Don't you understand, my boss needs more money. Bills to be fed, FICO score needs new debts so I can one day pay "them" for a 500,000 dollar shack plus 450,000 in interest until I'm 70.

I love her and she's mad at me. Could I take this every day for say the next 40 years. Her being hurt. My fucking it up. If she didn't love me back it'd be OK. That would be *normal* but having a chance and then having to *do something*. Don't you understand. I have to get gas go to the dermatologist follow up on my car loan fix my book cover... how could I leave this all behind. What if she came here. What if I could no longer jerk off alone at night then sift through piles of old mail.

My one chance. No question. Her laugh erased every *red pill* I ever choked down. I'd give her the divorce money. My kidneys

to eat. Keep this feeling. I need to stay crazy. Real enough that other women are fake, nothing, her voice makes them repulsive like putrid meat, like fresh piss in an elevator. They make me sick. This is love and she's in fucking Portugal and that thought intrudes. You love her because you can't have her. Don't you understand, it's a bad idea. It's "your alcoholism" that makes you want this. I don't care. I'll drink my way through it. Who can say what God wants.

Don't you understand I need to suffer and die alone. She's the one. No one else will be like this. Maybe I go and she eats me alive. No being rational. It's go or not. This is what teenage runaways feel. I'm 43. You don't lose it. What would it be like to feel this, and to have what you want be possible.

We'll never know.

Norwood

1.

In December a boy was born. Healthy and beautiful. His father looked up. Smiling until he saw the man waiting by the window. Gaunt in a black suit black hat. White hair. The man looked at the father. Then the boy. Then the father again. Tipped his hat and was gone.

2.

His new bathroom had two mirrors facing each other, and one morning he saw a bald spot. Right on top of his head at the... what was it called. Right at the *whorl*.

Or maybe it wasn't. His new bathroom had a bright light. He was going gray. Maybe just a light patch. He leaned in to the front mirror to look at the back mirror, instinctively. His reflection in back leaned away. Fuck.

He walked naked into the dining room, found his phone, walked back into the bathroom with his nuts huddling up in the cold. Leaned into the front mirror. Unlocked his phone with his thumbprint. Opened the camera app. Held the phone behind his head. It showed the ceiling. He brought the phone back down, switched to the reverse facing *selfie* camera, held it behind his head again. Guiding himself by the reflection of the camera in the front mirror. There. Perfect-with his left index finger he reached up to press the white virtual button to take the picture. His right hand instinctively went to move the camera closer to his left. Got a blurry and unflattering shot of his nose in the back mirror. It looked enormous.

Holding the backwards camera in the backwards mirror with his backwards hands it took ten tries to get it. But this was important. Finally there it was. Pink meat under hair. Was it a bald spot.

It wasn't *not* a bald spot.

3.

He looked again. After he'd dried off and got dressed. But he'd put on too much Aesop Parsley Seed Antioxidant Under-Eye Serum. It had got in his eyes and now he couldn't see. Everything was blurry. The picture was blurry.

It cost $85 for one fluid ounce. Ten eye droppers full. But he'd got a tester from the girl. She worked there. She'd brought him gifts, before she decided to be monogamous with the boyfriend who borrowed rent money and gave her chlamydia.

4.

The Joe Rogan Experience on YouTube played targeted ads on episodes where Joe didn't advocate drug use. LOSING YOUR HAIR? SKIN? MUSCLE? One said. FIGHT! THERE IS A SOLUTION.

LOS ANGELES AREA. NORWOOD MEN'S CENTER.

He clicked. A pop up said MAKE AN APPOINTMENT NOW. He didn't.

The ads followed him for nine months.

5.

He liked to take dates birdwatching, in the daylight before he got tired, but she insisted. It will be cool. It's a great art gallery with a bar and a happy hour. I *never* go on one on one first dates, she said. My friends will be there.

She was 32. They'd matched on Hinge. A Creative Executive for Netflix. He'd hoped to talk to her about *The Witcher*. Its surprisingly intelligent structural choices. Her profile said she wanted a yard for a dog. Which meant she didn't have one. Which meant he had a chance. Something red and itchy had been growing on his face under his eye. He'd been smearing ointment on it that got on his clothes but it kept growing. Maybe staying out of daylight was smart.

The bar was dark but a beam from a *light sculpture* made his ointment shine like a jewel. She didn't work on *The Witcher*. Her friends made more money than him designing *experiential marketing* for documentary series from the Obamas. He tried to say something. Without him even seeing that they moved the girls formed a sort of phalanx. Suddenly he was looking at her back in a cashmere sweater with BLACK LIVES MATTER on the front. She was rapt while a filmmaker for *Vice* talked about his six months sailing through diminishing Arctic sea ice.

6.

The Norwood Men's Center was in Glendale by the Forest Lawn cemetery. The graveyard had an art exhibit where he'd taken a date to a famous mural of Golgotha. The office was modern. The receptionist was hot. Maybe Filipina. Her name tag said *Sophie*. Sheer white shirt. Aqua color bra underneath. The first natural color hair he'd seen in weeks. Welcome to The Men's Center, she said. You have an appointment-

Hi, yes. He gave his name. Let me give you my Blue Cross–

We don't take insurance.

OK–like how much will it be

I can't give information about the cost in advance, sir. The doctor may discuss it with you. She handed him the clipboard. The forms.

OK is it more than ten thousand dollars?

I can't give information in advance

A hundred thousand?

I can't–

I'm joking, it's fine. How is it working here

It's good, I have time to study. I can write my papers–

Do the old guys hit on you, he said. The pen skipped halfway through writing "44" next to AGE. They'd asked him for his birth date. Why couldn't they just figure it out.

Sometimes, she said, and almost laughed.

What papers are you writing–

It's about a book called *Dogeaters*–about fighting patriarchy in the Philippines–

I've been there, he said. Thinking *good luck.* Picturing the woman with two black eyes wading through rice fields on a water buffalo.

I always wanted to go, she said.

You should. Your family's from there? Nakaka intindi ka ba ng Tagalog?

Haha, no. Maybe you can tell me about it. She was leading him into a corridor with wine color walls and posters for Semen Cryopreservation. Gestured him into a room. Can you please take off all your clothes, she said. You can fold them on the chair. Your underwear too, everything. As she closed the door behind her and he peeled down his boxer briefs the waistband caught on him; he was half hard.

7.

Norwood didn't make him wait. As soon as he'd sat down with the weight of his balls crinkling up the cold butcher paper the old man came in. Black suit. Black hat. Long white hair almost like The Witcher. Gaunt face like a greyhound. Not tall but a quality about him. Like a Jewish version of the old man from *Phantasm.*

So you want to keep your hair, he said. Voice like fall leaves rasping on asphalt.

We'll I'm not sure I'm losing it–

Anything else?

My face. You can see there's this red on my skin–

Mm hmm. Let's look at the hair first. Can you pull it back please.

Like this?

Yes, good.

Dr. Norwood snapped on toothpaste color gloves. Pulled open a high cabinet. Took down a black briefcase. Unlatched it. Inside, on a black cushion, a sickle-shaped knife. I'll just need a sample, he said. Hold still please. And pull the hair back, all the way back. Dr. Norwood was holding his cheek. The skin of his palm only as warm as the air. I'll just take a little bit.

The knife swished by his temple and it felt like a bird was pulling him with sharp claws. Dr. Norwood help up a lock of hair. Salt and pepper with a little blood at one end.

Sorry but we need to analyze close to the root. Lean forward please–

What do you think so far.

Male pattern baldness is rated 1 to 7. 1 is a full head of hair. 7 is–well, we've all seen. All men are on a journey to 7. Some die before they get there. Can you lean forward please.

Norwood pivoted to the other side of the exam table. He felt fingers rooting by his *whorl* like a chimp looking for an insect. Yes, said Norwood. Yes, there's some loss of density here. I'll take a sample–

The sickle knife snicked. Felt like a squirrel bit him–how much loss of density, he said.

The scale is 1 to 7. You're on the verge of "3 Vertex". You can lean back.

Is 3 Vertex bad?

Well your wife won't be happy–

I don't have a wife.

Mmm hmm, said Norwood. Lean to the left please.

Are you gonna cut off more hair?

Just a little sample. How long have you had the psoriasis–

Is that what it is? It's–OW–it was like this for a year but only my forehead, now it's my cheeks and eyelids, it's starting to hurt–

Well I'm sorry to hear that. No cure I'm afraid.

Is there *treatment?*

There are creams, said Norwood. But that's at the surface level. The root cause is not clearly understood. It's thought to be an overzealous immune response to the body's own cells. Lean back please–

The knife. AHH! So my immune system is *eating my face*–

"Eating" isn't the right word, the action is additive. It's building painful lesions on to your face. It's taking over.

OK but–

As I said, not much we can do. But it does sometimes fade.

It does?

Yes, and then comes back; the overall pattern gets worse over time of course. But you may have some good days. Can you lean to the right please.

Are you going to–

Just a small sample. Most men have no problem with it. Please just relax. Have you had decreased libido, loss of physical strength–

No-

When we see inflammation like yours, it's sometimes secondary to a decline in testosterone. It can be comorbid with impotence–

I mean, my sex drive is normal. It's powerful in fact–AHH! The knife like a snakebite.

You may find your experience changing.

Can I stop chasing women?

Desire never goes, said Norwood. Only what we desire goes. Open your mouth please.

Why?

I'm assessing the situation, be patient. I'll check the nose as well– Norwood's thumb began furiously bruising his gums– as

men age our noses and ears never stop growing. You can see for example, older members of the British Royal Family, it's quite hideous. And yours is abnormally large, disjointed– I'll take a look, but first–

The knife again. Back of his head. Like a cigarette put out on his skin.

How much hair do you need–

I need to make a full diagnosis. Now the nose please– tilt your head back–

His neck didn't want to move. He flinched like Norwood might cut his throat. But he leaned back. Norwood produced what looked like a small chrome drain snake. Try to relax, he said.

Norwood jammed the cold marble-size metal end into his nostril and began jerking the steel into his sinus. It felt like drowning. Thin fingers grated hard on his psoriasis patches. Made them sting. The bones in his face creaked like an old house in the wind. NNMMMPPH, he said.

It's as expected, said Norwood. Now for your testicles–

No–

It's for your own good, I need to understand your endocrine function.

He looked as Norwood brushed aside his paper gown, to where his nuts lay in their hideous pool of skin.

Quite distended, said Norwood. Are they always like this?

I guess.

At your age the gonads will have lost some function. Your sperm– what's left– may be… less than ideal. And the decline will of course continue. No wife no children?

No, guess I better get married quick.

To whom, said Norwood.

Is Sophie single?

I don't think she'd be interested in someone like you.

I was joking–

We joke when we're afraid of the truth, said Norwood. One more–

Before he could duck the sickle knife scraped halfway across his crown. It felt like being scalped by a tomahawk. Norwood dropped hair into what looked like a biohazardous waste bag.

What can you do about my hair–

What can we do about anything, said Norwood. Chuckled a little as he latched his knife case closed. Tucked it under his arm and reached for the door handle. But you'll be hearing from us. We'll see you again. Soon.

His scalp burned as he struggled into his pants. Stumbled into the hall. Lurching past the FREEZE YOUR SPERM poster he saw his reflection in the black letters. The dome of his skull naked and white. A few sickly spikes of bleeding gray hair.

Huge nose purple and jagged. Lakes of beet red wrinkling beneath his eyes. Sophie at the desk, startled, then breathing as if to calm herself. Something in her eyes like pity for a second. Then nothing.

I'll take your payment, she said.

The Red-Whiskered Bulbul

I went to pray this morning, looking out the front window. In the front yard the grass has gone to seed. A little wren came. And then finches with red faces, I don't know what they are. Landing on the foxtail grass making it sway under their little weight. Throwing their heads back to swallow the seeds. They inspect the weeping ficus I have outside in a pot. Investigate the undersides of the leaves. Maybe looking for aphids. A female hummingbird, a rufous or Allen's hummingbird, perching on the ficus branch, fluffing her neck, stretching out her long exotic tongue. You can hear the mourning doves out back. The mockingbirds. Ravens with their tock-tock sound like that hollow ribbed wooden thing you rubbed with a stick in music class in third grade. Not so bad. Power lines come down from my house, down the hill to the street, and the other day the rare red-whiskered bulbul landed there and looked at me. He was with his four children. I was afraid he'd die alone. But he caught a break.

The Spirit

One morning there was a girl on the Gold Line. Chinatown to Pasadena on the way to work. Office with no windows. Five years.

She was Japanese. He could tell by her sounds. She was crouching on the seat across from him. Squinting at a sign over a fire extinguisher making inchoate moans. She sounded like she was in one of their weird pornos. Soothing a businessman, cooing at him some reason she needed to take his pants off in the conference room to giggle at his small dark pixellated cock. It was September. A hundred degrees. Hadn't rained in five years. People couldn't flush the toilet or water their grass. Even industry might have to cut back. NPR said the water came from some giant cave under Colorado. Now it was gone. Pitch black empty air the size of a state, walls smeared with skin jelly from dying blind cave eels.

A hundred degrees and every day the sky the color of oil smoke. She had on a striped tank top and short black cotton shorts too big in the leg and when she crouched he could see her pubic hair in the shadows. Ooooooonnnhhhh, she said. She studied the fire extinguisher. Then looked at him. Her eyes black like a startled cat, all pupils. The train bumped around a curve.

He'd had a Hinge date once who worked in the record industry. Part of her job was shepherding teenage Japanese pop acts. The girls came to LA and took acid in public. Posted broken English Craigslist ads looking for black American boyfriends. Got raped. Yes their comic books are wild, she said, but they have

no concept of danger. Where they're from you can sleep on the street.

Ooooooooo-uh, whispered the girl.

She was beautiful. Even her jagged teeth made her approachable. You need an imperfection.

Hi, he said. It was an effort. His laptop was open. A story about some part of work he hated. About growing old alone.

She didn't move, just stared with her all black eyes. Smiled a little. Ooooooooonnnh... With her palms on the seats next to her she rocked on her haunches. Then she climbed down on all fours, scampered across the aisle like a monkey as the train thumped around another curve and sped up. And she climbed into the seat right next to him. The skin of her arms hot. He could feel it.

Hi, yeah... he said.

She was crouching again. Facing him. Looking into the side of his eyes and he felt her breath on his neck. She was four foot eleven, with that blueblack hair around her shoulders. She picked up her left hand and held out her thumb and finger and gently brushed a lock of hair out of his face. Kept her hand there behind his ear. Just looking at him. She exhaled and it swept into his dress shirt collar and tickled his collarbones. He didn't move his face. Just his eyes to see if anyone was looking. The car mostly empty. One diabetic black lady sleeping, snoring with sounds like a Tasmanian devil ripping apart bush meat.

Aaaaaahhhh, the girl whispered. He could smell her a little. It made him feel hot and cold.

Aaaaaahhhhh....

He didn't want to close the laptop. It might startle her. Might make her move, which he should want, but didn't. Hello, he said. Her hand was still but the train bumping made his hair travel between her fingers and it tickled him in a way that felt hypnotizing. Aaaaahhhh. She pursed her mouth a little when she breathed out again and blew cool right on his neck.

He took his right hand off the keyboard. Slid it behind her. She didn't move. Might have smiled a little. He put his hand on her back. Hot and damp through her thin tank top. She put her other hand on the other side of his face and it felt like there was chi moving through her palms. Ooooooohhhhh, she said.

Was the diabetic still asleep. Yes. There was the shuddering growl of her snot. Is this wrong. Is she intoxicated. Can she not consent. Should I be thinking about her killing me. One leg of her shorts popped open, her blueblack snatch hair, he could smell her a little, like baby ointment. Oooohhh, she said. He kissed her. Her cool top lip, her soft gentle mouth. He ran his hand down her back and she arched under it like a shelter kitten petted for the first time. He was thirsty. Worried his mouth would be dry. He was so hard it hurt. FILLMORE AVENUE, said a recording of a cunt on the loudspeaker. His stop.

He pulled back. She did too. Her black, black eyes. He looked toward the door. Closed his laptop. She frowned. Like she might cry. The diabetic woman grunted. Stirred. Rustled plastic

shopping bags that said I AM REUSABLE as the brakes screamed and the train shook to its stop. Lord, said the woman as she heaved herself up and shuffled crabwise toward the doors that grudgingly *shushhhed* open. He could read her T-shirt. It said:

If you take one step toward God
God takes two steps toward you

He waited.

Waited.

He let the door *shushhh* closed.

For just a second, out the Lucite window, he saw the long gray sidewalk to his office with no windows. The woman with her bags and her God shuffling forward. The train rattled like it was going over a big bump. And the sidewalk and the office were gone.

Ooohhhh, whispered the girl. Her breath made a noise like a calm warm ocean in his ear. Her tiny fingers twisting open his buttons. Her wet mouth on his neck and it felt like every hair was trying to climb off him. He could smell her. She climbed on his lap, her weight as light and gentle as a pet rabbit, and kissed him on the forehead like he was a baby and she was soothing him. Wrapped her legs around him and pressed the arches of her feet into the small of his back. Oddly rough for a city girl. His cock pushing on his thigh felt hot like a fever that made you speak gibberish.

The last stop was Sierra Madre, by the foot of the Angeles Crest. No one went there now. The national forest was closed from the fires and the gangs had been dumping bodies off the hiking trails. The train made sounds like thunder and his phone dinged and he knew it was his boss without looking. Ahh-ahhhh, said the girl, staring at him with her black eyes. Her baby ointment smell. The doors *shushhed* open. PLEASE EXIT THE TRAIN, said the cunt, and the girl stood up and ran out of the car barefoot like a startled faun. On the platform she stopped and looked back expectantly.

He followed.

She hurried through the commuter parking lot full of Kia Sorrentos for Inland Empire commuters headed downtown. He followed as she hopped a corral fence by a dusty ravine filled with dying sagebrush and creosote. Hotter than a hundred degrees and the air thicker somehow, even higher up. Clouds lower. He'd get about ten feet from her and she'd stop, looking back, just smiling, and then dart up the hard packed empty creek bed. He followed. Up, up past the backs of slumping bungalows toward the treeline where the streets ended. Wait, he said. Where are you going. She let him get close. He was sweating and she put her face to his neck and inhaled long and deep. Oooohhhh, she said, and turned around and ran again.

Maybe a mile up in the mountains she let him catch up. The chaparral had opened up and the the skeletons of burnt out Douglas firs spiked out of the dirt. She was in a patch of bare earth on a big crag of sandstone, looking back expectantly. Behind her a redwood tree black at the base from the fires. High as a big church clock tower with one green branch living. Here

before men came. Oil smoke color clouds moving, taking on strange shapes. A black phoebe perched on a dead tumbleweed, swaying on a stalk in the hot wind. It too was looking at him. High in the tree a pair of squirrels had stopped. He saw a raccoon's eyes under a tree trunk split in half by lightning strike. Coyotes, gray against the rocks. All watching.

The girl had her back to the redwood tree. She waved. *Come.*

He was panting when he got to her. He went to kiss her and she held his face away with her palms on his cheeks. Slowly turned him so his back pushed into the rough deep furrows of the redwood bark. Only then did she let him near her mouth. Her soft cool tongue. Her hands pushing his dress shirt open and his V neck Hanes Beefy Tee up to his chest and he felt his belt choking his guts for a second while she got the buckle off, opened his pants, pulled down his underwear and he was naked in the daylight. So hard it hurt. She pushed her tank top up and slid her naked belly on him. She was pulling down her shorts and he could smell her. She was pushing him down on the roots and climbing over him. He was inside her and she was moving, afraid it would end fast-- oooohhhh, she said. His hands were on her back pulling her down onto him and then they were gone. His mouth was gone. Her skin was rough and hard and alive and the clouds had voices he could hear murmuring. Cool rain roaring and hissing in the branches above him and around him. Stay still, she seemed to say. Stay still. Warm and wet as her face got close and her black eyes took up the sky and his toes reached into the dirt. No more sound but the wind whispering up high, as he curled himself into the Earth and drank.

delicioustacos.com

Cover drawing: owencyclops.com

From a painting by Maerten de Vos, 1572

Cover design: mattlawrence.net

Also by Delicious Tacos:

Hot Naked Tits

The Pussy

Finally, Some Good News